ROOM EMPTY

SARAH MUSSI

ROCK THE BOAT

Disclaimer: nothing in this story is representative of any person or institute.

A Rock the Boat Book

First published in Great Britain and Australia by Rock the Boat,
an imprint of Oneworld Publications, 2017

The moral right of Sarah Mussi to be identified as the
Author of this work has been asserted by her in accordance
with the Copyright, Designs and Patents Act 1988

ISBN 978-1-78074-974-7
ISBN 978-1-78074-975-4 (ebook)

Typeset by Hewer Text UK Ltd, Edinburgh
Printed and bound in Great Britain by Clays Ltd, St Ives plc

This book is a work of fiction. Names, characters, businesses,
organizations, places, and events are either the product of the author's
imagination or are used fictitiously. Any resemblance to actual
persons, living or dead, events, or locales is entirely coincidental.

Oneworld Publications
10 Bloomsbury Street
London WC1B 3SR
England

Stay up to date with the latest books,
special offers, and exclusive content from
Oneworld with our monthly newsletter

Sign up on our website
oneworld-publications.com

For the still suffering addict

FLIGHT ONE

SERENITY AND ACCEPTANCE

STEP ONE
POWERLESS AND UNMANAGEABLE

1

I remember the ad. It changed everything.

Greetings. If you've found your way to this page, it means you're looking for answers. That's a good sign. We may have some for you.
We're the highly successful Daisy Bank Rehab Centre.

We can help treat your addiction issues around:
- Alcohol dependency
- Amphetamine
- Cannabis
- Cocaine
- Crystal meth
- Dual Diagnosis
- Eating disorders
- Ecstasy
- Gambling

- Heroin
- Ketamine
- Mental disorders associated with addiction
- Mephedrone/MCAT/Miaow Miaow
- Methadone
- Prescription medication
- Process addictions
- Sex addictions

We cater for fourteen clients (ten private and four state funded).

We have single and shared rooms.

We're based in a lovely rural location.

We work solely with those under twenty-five.

We support the client in restoring their physical, mental and emotional well-being.

Our treatment programme incorporates the Twelve-step Process.

We guide the client towards an acceptance of their addiction.

We teach them to let go of the past and deal with problems in the here and now.

We value ourselves.

We can recover.

We are worth it.

2

My name is Dani. I am anorexic.

I'm a state-funded, residential client at Daisy Bank Rehab Centre.

I've lived most of my life in care.

I'm seventeen.

I'm hungry all the time.

I'm trying hard to eat.

I wrap my arms around my ribs and hug my Thinness to me. It is mine. All mine.

I know I'm underweight. Tony tells me this. He tells me to embrace recovery. I must eat more. I feel I eat too much. Tony says that's because I have a serious life-threatening illness, which includes Body Dysmorphic Disorder.

I am anorexic because I am dangerous.

If I really let myself eat, I wouldn't be able to stop. I would just be one big open mouth. I would swallow up every thought and feeling and action. I know that is a logical fallacy. Tony says so. He suggests that it is really love and connection

5

I'm looking for. But I do not think so. I think about food. Mountains of it. I would be one big bottomless belly. I would become morbidly obese. I would swallow up every single digestible thing in the world and everyone else would starve to death.

I cannot allow that to happen.

}

It's been a week since Carmen died, and I met the real Fletcher.

I'd known the fake Fletcher for much longer, of course.

It was at Carmen's funeral.

We are all fakes, aren't we? Probably Carmen was the biggest.

Up until they sent her into the inferno, Fletcher was just a fellow client, a phoney, self-serving crackhead, albeit someone I was supposed to pair up with. My recovery buddy, apparently. I'm not sure why the programme insists on the term 'buddy'.

They say Carmen took handfuls of pills. Mostly aspirin.

Maybe it's because the word 'buddy' isn't quite 'friend' but it's friendlier than 'partner' – partner sounds like a lover you don't love.

How many aspirin does it take to kill you anyway? Is there a ratio of grams to body weight?

How many calories are there in one aspirin? This was one thought I had as Fletcher grabbed hold of my arm.

Fletcher is an addict. We are all addicts of one kind or another. His kind is cocaine. Mostly. I like him. I think he likes me. He also likes crystal meth. He wears cute jeans. He's one of the 'cool' kids on the programme. He drinks Red Bull. Full sugar. He says it's the last bit of buzz he's allowed.

Do you think she counted the aspirins and added an extra handful, just to be sure?

Fletcher tugs at my arm. I wonder if he feels my Thinness. I'm not sure I want to share it.

'Don't,' he says. 'Don't keep on going over it.'

But I have to. Today I'm preoccupied by the Moment Of Death. I want to spin beyond it and see into the darkness.

To date, Fletcher and I have sat down and shared our strengths and weaknesses. That's all. Fletcher is also state funded. His strength is being considerate. Mine is having a lot of self-control. His weakness is pretty girls.

Apparently she vomited them all back up anyway. That must have been a blow. Suddenly the universe offers you another chance, just after you've taken a lot of trouble to be very sure it doesn't.

My weakness is that I don't think I'm pretty. If I had been prettier somebody might have adopted me. I want to be pretty. But I'm not – I never will be on the inside. If I was a bit thinner I might be. I also might be dead. That is not something I want to be, today. I lied about my weakness to Fletcher. I told him that I think I'm an Alien. It didn't matter, because until Carmen died I hadn't taken the whole recovery buddy thing seriously.

Addiction makes us all liars.

After she vomited, she took her scarf and hanged herself from the upstairs landing. She must have tied one end to the banister, noosed the other round her neck and jumped into the stairwell. Just to be very sure that time.

Do you think, on the way down, just before the Moment Of Death, she regretted it?

Fletcher tugs at my arm again. 'We need to talk,' he says.

I know we do. Carmen was the poster girl for Daisy Bank Rehab Centre. I liked her. The fake her, I mean. She had industrial-strength tips on how to get clean, be clean, stay clean. How to trust in your Higher Power (whatever you consider it to be), even when you can't trust anyone around you, including yourself. You always have to add '(whatever you consider it to be)' in brackets when you refer to the Higher Power. I have a problem with that. It offers too much choice. Fletcher says his Higher Power was the Buzz. He's had to find another one. I'm never quite sure what to choose.

It's funny, on the day she was going to graduate and check out into the world again, she chose not to. She chose to check out altogether. The Daisy Bank Group who invested in this centre must be well pissed. If *she* didn't make it, what are our chances?

'Dani,' hisses Fletcher, 'you're doing it again.'

'Doing what?' I mouth.

I'm dizzy with hunger.

'Your weakness.'

Only my second-best weakness. I shake my head, as if I really don't understand him. You can lie in so many ways.

'You're dislocating yourself from your feelings. You're being a goddamn Alien.'

'Goddamn' is the fake Fletcher's new favourite word.

How long does it take to die when you jump off an upper landing into a stairwell?

'Can't you see you're alienating yourself?'

Does your neck dislocate before you're strangled?

I look around. My legs feel weak. My knees look huge, jutting through the cloth of my jeans. The crematorium is all pale wood and pink light. Tinny music is playing. I would hate to spin into the unknown to the sound of electronic Pachelbel. I'd like pointy knees with shapely bits. But it doesn't really matter. Nearly everyone is crying/has cried/is sniffing/trying not to sniff. I'm just thinking about the Moment of Death and how long it takes, and if it hurts. And is there any peace beyond it? I also wonder if they're crying fake tears. After all, we only ever knew the fake Carmen. That much is apparent. So how can we cry for her? We might have hated the real one.

Suicide is relative, says Tony. Not eating is just another form of it.

Only it takes a lot longer and is far more painful.

4

Carmen's family are here. It's the first time I've seem them. They're all being admirably stoic. They sit apart from us addicts, lit up by a modern window of stained glass and the funeral director's supportive smile.

I'm glad they didn't see her after her Moment Of Death. It would have made it hard for them to be so serene. Her head was canted over far too far. I was confused. I grabbed her leg and shook it. Her leg was stiff. I thought it was some kind of joke. Her head flopped forward with a jerk. Her tongue poked out in outlandish style. I couldn't make it out.

Judith sits in front of us. She presses her hands together, not exactly in prayer, probably wondering why Carmen failed to prove Cognitive Behavioural Therapy infallible. That's Dr Judith Penrose, PhD (BACP Accredited), Psychodynamic Counsellor.

I like to think Carmen wanted me to be the first to find her.

Fletcher tries to direct-message me with a glance. It clearly says: This is such bollocks – this is why I hate the world.

11

Actually, the crematorium is very acceptable. It has magnolia walls, parquet flooring, institutional chairs, little black prayer books and a gateway to the beyond all arched out of reconstituted Cotswold paving.

That's why she chose that stairwell. She knew I used to creep down to the kitchens late at night and sit on the last step smelling traces of the food I'd refused to eat.

And they haven't stinted on the coffin. It's shiny with lacquer and has brass handles.

So her death was a special message to me. It said: I trust you the most. Find me before the others.

My hand came away from her leg wet.

The gateway to beyond has blue curtains. One solitary designer candle lights the way.

I went on down the stairs and sat on the last step. Supper had been lasagne and garlic bread. Something dripped off her shoe on to the step beside me. Followed by sticky toffee pudding.

Everything is very respectable here.

And the flowers are fake.

Fletcher hisses more than 'bollocks' at me. He's being inappropriately concerned, as if I'm taking all this very badly.

I went back up to my room and found a towel and some perfume. I wrapped the towel around her legs. It soaked up most of it. I rubbed, until her tights were clean and nearly dry. They only ripped a little. Then I wiped the stairs too. I sprayed her with Obsession, before I called Tony.

Thank God for silk and real-touch floristry.

I couldn't let her face us all in that state.

Fletcher is in a bad way so I follow him outside.

5

Fletcher Harris Taylor is now insisting that I talk. He has every right to do that. Outside is cold and concrete, and I'm not keen on talking. That's a lie. There are some white and purple crocuses. And the words inside me could drown the planet if I pulled the plug on them.

'Talk,' says Fletcher.

I'm shivering and imagining Carmen inside that coffin, burning. An Alien bursts out of the coffin lid and smiles. The Alien lasers me with a sonic beam. My skin turns to liquid. My insides pour out and flood. It's not pretty. And a lot of people drown.

''Bout what?' I say.

''Bout what?' he mimics.

I shrug.

'About everything,' he says.

The Alien waves and gets back into the coffin.

'OK.'

'OK?' he mimics again. 'Come *on*! Carmen died. She didn't make it. And she had family.'

'Maybe that was it,' I say. 'Maybe she couldn't stand them.'
Fletcher gives me a weird look.

'Go on, say it – "like I'd know".'

He shakes his head. 'So it's like that, is it?'

'Like what?'

'Dani Goddamn Alien Spencer. Today, tomorrow and for ever.'

I get his point. I'm being toxic.

I wonder what we'll have for lunch.

'Toxic' is Tony's best favourite word. Everything is toxic. Society is toxic. Self-hate is toxic. Crosstalk is toxic. Negativity is toxic. Addiction is toxic. Not that I'm going to eat it. Tony says anorexia is definitely toxic. Virtually no part of the body escapes its effects. Fifty percent of all anorexics have low white-blood-cell counts; thirty-three percent are anaemic. Whichever way you look at it, the anorexic's immune system is seriously compromised. Practically no resistance to disease.

Disease is toxic.

I am already diseased.

Tony says I should talk about my disease. And Not Talking is toxic. But I don't want to talk.

'She's dead, Dani. She's not going to be around ever again.'

'Death has its attractions,' I say. I'm not going to let Carmen down.

I think Fletcher might punch me. I'd like that. He has supernaturally lovely, punch-throwing shoulders. And a good punch would hurt less than talking.

He punches me. He says, 'You've been in rehab for eight weeks and not put on an ounce. That's not recovery.'

I take my corner: I have put on an ounce. Actually, I've put on four. I'm trying to eat. I cut out my morning workout. I'm doing better than you. I'm doing better than Lee (everyone is doing better than Lee). It's not my fault. I've never been loved. You try that. I can drown you. If I'd had a proper start . . . It's all right being you. It's easy for you. You're not ugly. You're a crackhead, and a phoney-fake person.

And an eating disorder is the most difficult addiction to quit.

Fletcher delivers a right hook. 'And you don't try in meetings. You just don't.'

'How do you know?'

How *does* he know? It's OK for him to talk in meetings. He's got a motor engine for a mouth; it just goes on and on spitting out toxic fumes.

Fletcher flexes and circles round me. 'And don't do the denial thing. Not here. Not now. This is serious, and I need a real sparring partner or I'm not going to make it. So cut out all the defensive shit.'

It's all about him as usual. God, crackheads are so self-obsessed. What about me?

'Even in your head.'

And then he grabs my Thinness again and steers me away from the crocuses towards a tree. There are tiny leaf buds on the tree. There are two graves behind it.

Fletcher delivers his knock-out punch: 'You're ugly, and you'll stay ugly until you choose not to be. We need to talk. Think about it and let me know.'

15

6

I do let him know. I send him a text after we get off the shuttle bus. When we're all back at Daisy Bank Rehab Centre. The bus was laid on for all of us, so that we could achieve closure.

Meet me in Carmen's old room.

It will be empty. Until the new person comes. There's bound to be extended Circle Time tomorrow.

It seems the right place. I hesitate. Carmen would've wanted us to. She would've liked that. Lunch was a buffet of cold meat and warmed up quiche with salad. She trusted me. She believed in recovery buddies. And talking. And I didn't let her down. Though she also didn't like the word 'buddy'. She thought it was affected. 'But forget the language of recovery,' she said. 'It's being real with just one other human being that heals. You can call them whatever you want.' She was always a never-ending source of strength.

We can talk without being interrupted there.

I wonder if Judith phoned ahead, when we left the crematorium, to let them know when to warm up the quiche.

It's nice to do something Carmen would've liked. Although it doesn't matter, of course, if she would have liked it or not. She's dead.

1

Daisy Bank Rehab Centre is in Berkshire. It's just a quick drive away from Ascot. You can visit your recovering child on your way back from the races. It's also handy for Windsor and Eton. Fletcher did not go to Eton. Though O'Higgy did. That's Fion Cormac O'Higgins, gambler, but he got stuck with the iggy bit. Everyone calls him Iggy. Poor him.

Life isn't a game of tennis. That's what Judith says when we complain of being stuck with things. Don't expect it to be. Iggy knows all about that.

Anyway, the centre has a lovely garden at the rear, old urns, ornate gazebo, trailing climbers, and it's a grand old house: five storeys of London brick and a stucco edifice. It has two staircases. The front one, which is broad and impressive, and the back one, where Carmen hanged herself.

There have been other tragic events at Daisy Bank. They won't struggle to fill her place. But it may mean they'll keep their fees competitive. I don't think that's why Carmen did it, obviously, but that would have pleased her. It's funny how we

18

think so often of pleasing the dead. When Carmen was alive nobody tried to please her. She was always the one being agreeable. Her buddy was a total jerk.

Though to be fair, the staff at the centre are always pleasant. They talk to you in grave, kindly voices as if you've been naughty but are forgiven. When you complain about the way life dealt you a shit hand, they always have a soothing answer.

When you tell them that the care system doesn't care and should be renamed, they say, 'But they arranged for you to come here, and that was a very caring thing to do, wasn't it?'

And that shuts you up, because if you say 'no' then it means this place is shit, and if you say 'yes' then it means you were mistaken about how uncared for you felt.

And that is a very pleasant little dilemma.

For someone who is an Alien.

💣 ☠ 👎

That evening we meet in Carmen's room. It's quite empty. All her stuff is gone. But it still smells of her. That's strange: how your smell doesn't die with you.

Fletcher is late. He bangs into the room and he's sweating.

'Sorry,' he says. 'It's Lee.'

That's Lee Darren Grant. Fletcher's recovering junkie roommate, who is not trying to recover.

I don't say anything.

'He wants me to cover for him again at supper.'

'And will you?'

He shrugs. 'No choice.'

'Everyone has a choice. That's what all this is about.'

'Yeah. Like you've ever lived on the streets.'

'But we aren't on the streets.'

'Once you've lived there, it's not so clear-cut.'

'Well, that's your choice.'

He sits down on the bed. His punch-throwing shoulders slump. I must try to be kinder.

'I know,' he says. 'But you should shut up.'

Perhaps I should not try to be kinder.

'Because you talk about choice, but that's all rhetoric. You're buying into their rhetoric.'

'You should shut up yourself. You're not helping Lee by covering for him. If he doesn't want to get better, he shouldn't be here. He's using up a place that could be sponsoring someone else.'

'It's always so goddamn black and white with you, isn't it?'

Actually, I should shut up. I can see he's upset, and I'm feeling faint. And I know he needs a real sparring partner. But I can't. I want to bait him. I imagine breaking off a tiny crust of quiche and rolling its crumbliness between my fingers. There's something about an argument that makes me come alive. The Alien stirs, opens a score of eyes, sends out long antennae.

'We're really lucky to be here, to have a state-funded place at a lovely centre like this.' I know just how to wind him up.

He stiffens. 'Lucky?'

'Yes, lucky! For every state-funded kid here, there are a thousand out there that didn't make it.'

I put on a subtle, saccharin voice. I work in the words 'state

20

funded' as often as possible. It tells him he is nothing. He is nobody. He has a failed family. He's poor. He's an addict. He's broken. He must take handouts. He must do what they say. If he doesn't, they will sling him out. And he'll have to go back to being scum. He must say, 'My name is Fletcher. I am an addict. I am a broken creature who will never recover.' Over and over. To the very establishment that broke him. He must be grateful to them, grateful that they are willing to offer him a repair job.

You see, I haven't forgiven him for calling me 'ugly'.

'Oh, Dani,' he says.

He's a shell now, fragile as a dried sea urchin. His shoulders implode. Good.

'Carmen is dead,' he says. His eyes pass through me, pass through the walls of Daisy Bank Rehab and out over Berkshire. 'She was the only one who made sense.' His voice hollows out. 'I need help. I'm not getting better. I'm barely staying clean. I'm scared. I need you to be there for me.'

And I melt. The Alien dissolves into a mess of gooey green sludge. All its eyes blink out. Its antennae snap.

And I pull the plug.

'OK,' I whisper. Because that is the thing about being real. It has a power beyond anything in the universe and all Aliens shun it.

'You'll help me?'

'Yes.'

'To beat this thing?'

'Yes.'

'All the way?'

'Yes.'

'Whatever I do – even if it's shit?'

'Yes.'

And I will. I will. That's all. I will, and he will be my own Fletcher. And I will be there for him, even unto death.

Fletcher sighs like at last, after seventeen years, he can breathe. I reach out my hand. He takes it. He kisses the back of my fingers. He kisses them like he's a knight in shining armour pledging his life. I know what he's saying. His kiss tells me that he will be there for me too. All the way. Through the dragon fires of hell.

A shiver runs up my arm. 'But if I'm going to do that, I'll need to recover a bit,' I say. 'I'm not really very strong. Not up to *War of the Worlds* yet.' I display my non-existent biceps. I'm so hungry. 'I lied about the four ounces, you know.'

'Then you must recover,' he says.

'OK.'

No one drowns.

He smiles.

It's too bright in here. Suddenly. In Carmen's room. Some junkie feeling, like her spirit is smiling. I don't know how to survive in a solar system without Aliens. It feels too real. I've grown used to the cold of Outer Space. I'm not ready yet. Not ready for any kind of life form.

'This is way too much reality.'

I need fakery for just a teeny bit longer.

Fletcher feels it too. He laughs, straightens up.

'You're goddamn right,' he says.

STEP TWO
RESTORE US TO SANITY

8

You are not allowed to think I am in love with Fletcher. Once you have got the Thinness in your life, you don't need love any more. I'm not sure what real love is anyway. I'm not sure I've ever encountered it.

Unlike conditional love.

That is the kind of love you can trust.

It has a glorious elegance all of its own.

Just three easy-to-follow stages.

Stage One: I've got something you want; I'm prepared to swap it for your attention.

Really simple concept.

Warning: it can be tricky sometimes. For beginners. You have to decide: is that one smile, that word of encouragement, that feeling that somebody is on your side actually worth it?

Stage Two: don't fool yourself you have found the real thing.

The real thing doesn't exist.

23

Despite all the efforts of the Disney World Reality Channel to convince us otherwise. You know the one.

'Some Day My Prince Will Come.'

'You've Got a Friend in Me.'

'Once Upon a Dream.'

'You'll Be in My Heart.'

'True Love's Kiss.'

'Part of Your World.'

Stage Three: a deal is a deal, and you can expect to get paid on it, if you deliver.

I gave Fletcher my word that I would be there for him. So at Circle Time, I send my Alien back to Outer Space and zap Fletcher with an ultrasonic beam. He direct-messages me back: a small smile. His smile says: I am glad you remembered we have a deal.

Everyone is at Circle Time. There are thirteen of us plus the counsellor. There's one empty chair.

'The empty chair is there so that you can imagine Carmen sitting in it,' says Judith, like we are not addicts, just thick.

Everybody obligingly looks at the empty chair. I can't imagine Carmen sitting there. That's not because I can't imagine her. I can see her ripped tights and dangling legs very clearly. It's because there is absolutely no need to imagine her there; she's supposed to have left, so she wouldn't be in Circle Time. The fact that she chose to hang herself with an old scarf is irrelevant – she still wouldn't have been there.

'I want you all to take a moment to say goodbye to her in your own way,' says Judith.

Somewhere in Outer Space I can hear the Alien howling with laughter.

'We said goodbye to Carmen yesterday, at the funeral,' says Iggy. He's being pointedly obtuse. I like his logic. He's probably going to crack a joke working in the words 'dead right'.

And Carmen didn't say goodbye to us. Carmen didn't think we were worth saying goodbye to, so how does that compute?

'That is true,' says Judith in her I-am-a-counsellor-who-must-speak-in-a-very-smooth-and-mellow-rich-tone-in-case-you-have-guessed-I-am-better-than-you voice. 'But she was our special friend, so we must say goodbye to her in our special forum. Our Circle Time.'

Everybody looks at her blankly.

'Shall I say goodbye for us?' asks Judith.

She's noticed her closure ceremony is not going to plan. Sometimes I wish she would just say that. I wish she would say, 'This is sheer bollocks. I thought it was a good idea but it isn't and I'm winging it, so what shall we do instead?'

But when you're a Daisy Bank Rehab counsellor you can't do that.

I want to know what the point of recovering is if it turns you into a hypocrite?

If Carmen *was* here, sitting in that chair, she would say something just right, something that would fill the gap and make everyone relax without being too phoney.

The Alien farts.

I realize I'm doing Toxic Thinking.

I'm wishing Carmen were here to help us.

It's a kind of thinking that only an addict can do really well.

Imagining that the very person who caused the problem is the same one who can solve it. It's all part of your addiction.

The fart was called Long And Strong.

If you think like that, you're in deep shit.

You're like a worm caught on a hook, wriggling around, hoping that the person who stuck the barb into you will remove it.

I know – mad.

Plus Carmen was a classic people-pleaser and everyone knows that codependency is a slimy, cowardly thing despite all the good press it gets.

'When you've imagined Carmen sitting on the chair, you can decide what you would like to say to her so that we can let her go,' says Judith.

The Alien has a whole bouquet of farts.

Long And Strong.

Silent But Violent.

Loud And Proud.

He's trying to get my attention.

I know what's coming next. We'll have to go around the circle and everybody will have to say something fatuous and embarrassing to an empty chair.

He also has one called Hell Of A Smell, which is guaranteed to asphyxiate.

'When you're ready, we can start,' says Judith.

This is probably going to take for ever. I decide to get my turn over and done with, so that I can zone out until we do something less dreadful.

'My name is Dani. I am anorexic,' I say.

Everyone murmurs, 'Hi, Dani.'

'OK, Carmen,' I say. 'I'm sorry you had to kill yourself. I'm sorry you didn't love any of us enough to stick around. I'm sorry you thought killing yourself was a nice way to say good-bye to us. I suppose you wanted to show us, however hard we try, there is no hope. I'm pretty angry about that. I tried to be your friend. I thought you cared. I thought you actually liked me. Obviously you didn't. That makes you exceptionally hateful and an emotional liar. Worse – because you took advantage of me. It makes you someone I could never have been true friends with. And that makes me very sad. At least, I'm trying to realize that it makes me very sad. What I actually feel is very, very angry. So you can rot in hell for all I care. Because that was a very mean thing to do.'

'Thank you, Dani,' everyone murmurs.

That is the best I can do. Now I can zone out and add up jumping jacks and deduct calories. At least I've been honest. Unlike Judith. Today I have decided to be as real as possible, otherwise the Alien will get his way and win me over with well-timed farts. I have a deal with Fletcher. I've felt the power of connection. Today I am not happy to play with the Alien in Outer Space.

The circle goes quiet.

Who will be the next to speak?

The tension is quite exciting. I don't zone out straight away.

It's like a game – if you don't get in quickly, somebody else may say what you want to, and then you'll look like an idiot if you just say the same thing. You're supposed to be reflecting deeply upon your feelings – that's if you have any feelings

– and apparently you can't have the same feelings as somebody else.

However, experts now say that addiction is linked to Narcissistic Personality Disorder. That means addicts probably have no feelings they're able to acknowledge anyway. Everybody knows narcs think they're totally perfect. So that's really funny because it means all of Judith's theories about expressing repressed and difficult feelings are doomed. But I don't mention this to her. Therapists always have to feel they know better than you even though they don't. We have to be kind to them because they need to feel like they're doing a good job.

9

Of course it's Lee who breaks the silence. It would be. Only someone like Lee could make a comment that makes him the laughing stock of the entire circle and lets everybody else relax at the same time.

'Rest in peace, bruv, Carmen,' he says. 'Peace an' love an' rock an' roll foreva in da higher place. You will be missed. And always in our hearts. Oh yeah.'

Lee is an encyclopedia of insincere stock phrases.

He looks around the circle and grins at anyone whose eye he can catch. You're not supposed to look around the circle. You're not supposed to engage in crosstalk. Crosstalk is when you communicate directly with others in Circle Time. That's talking, farting or eye language. Judith says it impedes flow, makes us self-aware, stops us from genuine reflection.

No crosstalk is one of the first and most basic rules of Circle Time.

We are ecstatic Lee is engaging in it. That's because my

29

comment has made everyone feel uncomfortable. And *that* is what Tony calls a double bind.

A double bind is an emotionally distressing dilemma in which you can receive two or more conflicting messages, and one message negates the other.

You could say life is a good example of a double bind.

Here we're told to say whatever comes into our minds, to access our deep feelings, to give them voice. Tony says that is what heals.

But the subtext to that is you should not give voice to anything that makes others feel uncomfortable.

I can't be sure of that.

Because subtext is always unspoken.

The Alien has dressed up like a Victorian explorer and is holding up a placard which reads: *I AM OFF TO THE DARK SIDE OF THE MOON. COMING?*

But that's the nature of a double bind. It relies on subtext.

I think that's why Judith lets Lee get away with crosstalk. That's why nobody minds his scripted, banal comments. Everyone loves a loser.

The tension becomes unbearable. Who will be the next sucker to break it?

As long as Lee carries on losing, we can all feel we're winning.

It's Jennifer.

'My name is Jennifer. I am an addict.' I should have guessed she'd crack first. Jennifer has a lopsided haircut that constantly startles me.

'Hi, Jennifer,' everyone murmurs.

'We will miss you, Carmen.'

The group exhales.

'That's all,' says Jennifer. There's a catch in her throat. Like she's carried away with her own sentiment.

'Thank you, Jennifer,' everyone choruses.

She's such a big fraudster. She's just better at it than Lee. I don't think she will miss Carmen at all. She never sat down by Carmen at lunchtime, even if she wasn't point-scoring. She never seemed too bothered about hanging out with Carmen when she was alive. I don't think she would have said that if Carmen had just gone home to her family alive and well.

I want to break all the rules and turn on her and say, 'You're a vile, repulsive, bogus, sham dollop of shit. You're just think-ing about your own death – that's why you're getting all teary.' A sudden rage swells inside me, thick, choking, like smoke from a fire when damp leaves are thrown on it.

I mentally throw a lot more damp leaves on it.

Carmen was nothing to me.

I didn't even know her, did I? I must fight mood swings and impulsivity. If she had cared about me, she would not have hanged herself.

Nobody else wants to say anything. So we all just sit there and waste time. Everyone is trying to look like they are deeply meditating on the nature of life and death and being hung from the backstairs with an old scarf.

Judith saves the day. 'I'm going to pass round a card with aphorisms on it,' she says. 'Please choose an aphorism to read out.'

Judith picks up the card and reads out her best choice. 'Gratitude is an attitude, not a platitude.'

She passes the card to Carla.

'Self-esteem is not thinking of yourself more, but thinking more by yourself,' Carla says very prettily. She passes the card on.

'Man proposes, the Higher Power disposes,' reads out Iggy. It's Jennifer's turn.

Underneath all those leaves, a furnace is roaring. I could beam the Alien down from the Dark Side. He could flatulate all over her with deadly digestive gases from Jupiter. We could rake off the leaves and build her a funeral pyre.

'Don't think about acting, act on thinking,' Jennifer says.

I catch Fletcher's eye. His crosstalk is not cross. It's full of conditional love. The fire dies down until it's just a warm glow.

The aphorisms continue.

'Your worth comes from inside, not from outside.'

'Willing to be open and open to be willing.'

'O.O.P.S.,' chooses Lee. He grins shamelessly. 'Our Only Priority is Sobriety.'

'To keep what you have, you must give it away,' says Fletcher. His eyes are all flecked with light.

He passes the card to me. I'm trying to work out what he means.

I choose an aphorism at random. 'This too shall pass,' I say.

'Let it begin with me,' whispers Alice, the mousiest girl in the world.

'Good, better, best. Never let it rest till your good is better and your better is best.'

'Be brave enough to be scared.'

I'm still wondering what Fletcher was trying to tell me.

'Recovery is a journey . . . not a destination.'

That's it.

Life is a double bind because it's too painful to bear but you don't want to die.

I understand now.

My anger suddenly vanishes.

Carmen was just solving a dilemma.

10

'This morning's group session,' says Judith, 'is going to centre on Early Childhood Trauma.'

Early Childhood Trauma is a favourite of Judith's. She comes from the school of psychodynamic counselling that believes in Dredging Up Old Nasty Things that happened a very long time ago, possibly and preferably even before you could remember anything.

She doesn't share her theories with us, but simply explains that deep trauma received in early childhood leaves a scar on the psyche. The Child learns that the world is an untrustworthy place. If basic trust isn't established (according to Judith), that leaves the Child with no other conclusion to come to than to believe she is unworthy.

Judith always refers to the Child as 'she'. As if no baby boys are ever born in the psychodynamic analytical world.

As far as I understand it, if the Child cannot establish basic trust in the world, she will internalize that as Not Being Good

Enough. This will then become a self-fulfilling prophecy. And she won't be good enough at anything.

That's when the fun begins.

Every subsequent failure or disappointment will confirm to the Child that she's a waste of space. And so layer upon layer of hurt and trauma will be plastered over the original trauma. Until the Child is one horrible, screaming, internal mess.

It isn't very nice to think of my inner child as a horrible, screaming, internal mess. But Judith is convinced that is the root of my problems. In fact, it's the root of all our addictions. If we can get the inner child to stop screaming, and we can clear up the horrible mess, then we won't want to starve ourselves or smoke crack cocaine.

'I want you all to close your eyes,' says Judith.

We all close our eyes. Except Lee. He has a vested interest in not recovering, plus someone has to see how well we're doing.

'We're going to peel back the layers of the onion until we find the core,' says Judith.

I don't point out that apples have cores and onions only have centres and that educated psychodynamic counsellors should not mix their metaphors when dealing with vulnerable, inner-screaming children.

Today, I will be kind.

'I want you to go back in time to when you were very little,' says Judith. 'I want you to remember your earliest possible memory. I'll give you a few moments to find that memory.'

Judith gives us a few moments. It's really just a silence in which you can hear your tummy rumbling and everyone else doing spooky breathing. But today I'm going to try her therapy. Today I'm going to do it properly. If I am to help Fletcher – Fletcher of the light eyes and the punch-throwing shoulders – then I have to be stronger.

So I apologize to the Thinness and tell it that I haven't abandoned it. 'You are still my best friend,' I say. 'At all times you have helped me survive bad things. I will never forget you,' I promise. 'I will only recover just enough to function and be useful, and then I am all yours.'

Now I have permission to access my earliest memory.

The Thinness will always be my first friend and best friend.

Behind my eyes is a weird, grainy black screen with white dotty interference all over it. It's a bit like one of those analogue TV screens that won't tune in. I try to look into the screen to see what my earliest memory might be.

'Go back to your first day at school,' says Judith.

I remember my first day at school. I sat on a bench with some other kids and played with some blocks. There was a sand tray at the side of the room. I would have liked to play with that, but I wasn't sure I was allowed to. So I played with the blocks, which was a bit boring, because by the time you had balanced a few blocks on top of each other and they had fallen down a few times, you'd got the hang of it.

'I want you to go to an earlier memory now,' says Judith. 'What happened before your first day at school?'

I can still see the analogue TV screen behind my eyes. I'm going to try.

I go back to the place where I was living before I went to school. It was a children's home with a blue carpet in the playroom.

'Perhaps your earliest memory might be when you hurt yourself,' says Judith. 'Perhaps you fell over and bruised your knee.'

That actually helps. I can remember when one of the bigger kids elbowed me in the nose and I got a nosebleed. I lay on my back and somebody brought a bowl of water. It was a yellow bowl and they pressed a damp flannel over my nose and made me sit up. I had my nose pinched and that hurt.

'When you get to the earliest memory possible,' says Judith, 'I want you to stand up in your imagination. Please stand up. You don't need to leave your seats.'

I mentally stand up.

'I want you to imagine yourself in front of a door,' says Judith. 'It's a big door. It's made of heavy wood. Please reach out your hand and take hold of the door handle.'

I reach out my hand and take hold of the door handle.

'Please turn the door handle,' says Judith. 'Please push the door open; it will open inwards and away from you.'

I push the door handle down. The door opens inwards and away from me.

'Behind the door is a room,' says Judith. 'I want you to step through the doorway into the room. I want you to keep your eyes closed as you do this.'

I step through the doorway into the room. I keep my eyes closed. The room is very cold. It's so cold. I start shivering almost immediately. It smells horrible, like meat rotting. I can hear a fly buzzing.

The door slams to behind me.

'I want you to remember every single thing you see, hear, smell and feel. We'll use this information later to help you map your inner subconscious world,' says Judith. 'So now, inside your special room, open your eyes and look around.'

I'm scared. I don't want to be in this room. I don't like being this side of the door. *I promised Fletcher.* I don't want to open my eyes. I don't want to see what's here.

'Look around your room.'

I must try.

I have a deal.

I open my eyes.

I'm looking straight at a barred window. It's a window with four sections. In front of the grimy panes are three thick bars. The wall around it is painted cream. It's dirty. In one corner, beside the window, is an old frayed armchair, covered in a bobbly, raggedy, red material. It smells terrible. I can hear something in the distance, something banging around. The screech of gates – large, metal, heavy, opening.

'I want you to think very carefully now,' says Judith. 'I want you to ask yourself these questions: Are you alone in the room? Or is somebody else there with you?'

I'm shivering and shivering.

'Please look around your room and tell me who you are with,' says Judith.

I must try.

Fletcher.

Room Empty

I take my eyes away from the filthy glass of the window, away from the stained chair. On the floor is a threadbare carpet. I turn around to see who is in the room with me.

The Alien screams from the edge of the universe. I hear him in torment, raw, screaming.

I'm trapped.

On the far side of the room, stretched across the doorway, is a long, adult shape.

Slumped, stinking, bloated.

11

I can't get out.

Please help me.

I look at the body. My throat is dry. I stand in the room. I've screamed myself hoarse. I cross the floor. I'm very small. I think I've wet myself. I go nearer. I'm very hungry. My knees are shaking. My leg bones are all dissolved. My heart has gone. Not beating.

I catch hold of its shoulder. It's putrid. Soft. Maybe it's not dead.

I shake it.

Like a zombie, the arm falls limp.

I scuttle back. I don't know what to do. There's a pain in my stomach. I go to the farthest corner of the room, as far away as I can. I'm trembling. It's dead. I sit down. My chest is leaking, draining out through big holes. I pull my knees up to my chin. My face is falling off in great chunks. I curl into a tiny ball. I can poke my fingers through my flesh down to the skull. I push my eyes down on to the tops of my knees. My teeth are chattering. I can't stop shivering. I can't think what to do. I try to hold my cheeks on, jam them into the spaces of my jaw. I try to unravel the past. I want to go back to being someone else.

I'm alone.

Oh, help me.

Let somebody help me.

I lift my head up. A shadow falls across the room. Bits of dust are caught in a beam of light. The light is coming from somewhere. The body casts a shadow against the door. An extraterrestrial being floats down through the light into the centre of the room. He shakes the dust off himself and grins.

I cannot smile because my lips have gone. I raise one hand to show him I know he's there.

'You called for help,' he says.

My hand is all skeletal.

'I'll take care of you from now on,' he says.

I nod. I need someone to take care of me.

'I'll never leave you,' he says. 'Aliens don't die. So you can stop worrying about that.'

You might go back to your spaceship, I say. Except that I don't really say it; I just think it.

'True,' he says, 'but I can come back again whenever you want me. I can beam down straight into your mind.'

The Alien expands. He has tentacles. He has a large number of eyes, big like flying saucers. He looks a bit like a spider. And the tentacles have nasty-looking suckers on them. I don't like spiders. I'm scared of spiders. I want the Alien to stop waving his tentacles up and down at me.

'Don't be afraid,' he says.

But I am afraid.

'I'm your friend,' he says. 'I've come to help you. Wherever there are lost little children locked in rooms with dead bodies, the Aliens will come to help them.'

I nod my head. I know this is true.

'So please invite me to come in,' says the Alien, 'then I can live in your mind for ever.'

'OK,' I say. Except I don't have a voice because my tongue has fallen out through the hole under my jawbone. But I nod my skull at him. I would like to be friends. I want to say that I'm afraid of spiders. I want to ask him if he could be a bit different, but I'm too scared he'll go away and leave me alone with the body.

'Well done.' The Alien grins.

Then he pulls all his tentacles back in and blinks his eyes at me, and stands up very tall so that he looks huge. He bunches all his muscles up, until he looks like a great big jumping spider with no legs, and he takes a little scuffle across the floor and bounds straight at my face.

He slithers up the hole where my nose once was and slides into my brain.

12

I scream.

I scream and scream.

I jump to my feet. The chair falls over.

I have to get out. I have to get out of this room. I have to get out of all rooms. I just have to go.

You're not supposed to scream in Circle Time. If you have a problem with the exercise, you're supposed to hold up one hand, like you're at the dentist, to show you're in pain. Judith will then bring everybody back into the room, safely, and give you some time out.

I can't wait for her to bring everybody back. I can't wait for her to give me time out.

I race across the room. I yank the door open. I race down the corridor. I race past the pictures of distant mountains and woodland groves. I race past the yellow paint in the entrance to the refectory. I turn at the end of the corridor. I race down the stairs, past Carmen's legs, across the next landing and down the next set of stairs, past the sash window with the

43

beams of sunlight streaming in. And the dust is crowding into the bars of sunlight, swirling, as I race through it. Scarcely breathing, I race down the next set of stairs to the back door. I slam open the door and race down the steps into the garden.

I race across the patio. Jump down two stone steps. Past the stone with the trailing geraniums. Across the lawn. The dew on the grass soaks my shoes. Down past the pond. To the end of the garden, by the wall. I look up through the leaves of the honeysuckle and see the big blue sky. The infinite distance of space.

I'm shivering. I'm shaking. I'm breathing. I'm gasping. I can't think.

'Say the word and we can go up there right now,' says the Alien. He wraps a tentacle around my shoulder. 'We can be together.' Its suckers hold firm to my Thinness.

I feel sick. I tried so hard this morning. I drank a cup of tea. I nibbled a piece of toast. And even though I laboured my mouth dry, until the top of my tongue felt sore, I couldn't get enough saliva to work it properly. I managed to swallow the taste. Now my stomach is hurting. I feel ill. I start to vomit into the bushes where the azaleas grow. My stomach heaves and heaves, until it feels red and round and empty, like a bullet has passed straight through.

I pull the leaves off the trailing honeysuckle. I wipe my mouth with the back of my hand. I suck in air. I'm shaking. I try to understand what's happened. My heart is going so fast, I'm dizzy.

I went back into a memory.

And found a body.

44

I don't know why there should be a body.

But I've been in that room before. *Everything was so familiar.*

I'll never go back there again.

Never.

Never.

Never.

I'll shut it down. I'm not in that locked room any more.

I'm out.

I'm going to stay out.

I'll never ever go back into my memories again.

Never.

Even if it means I'll never recover.

'But you found me there,' whispers the Alien.

There was a body.

'And you know I'll never leave you.'

Why was there a body?

'The only place they can force me to leave you is in that room.'

The Alien tightens his hold. The suckers on his tentacles sink through my Thinness.

Right to my bones.

'So I'll make sure nobody ever tricks you into going there again.'

STEP THREE
OUR WILLS AND OUR LIVES

13

I can't stay in the garden.

They'll find me.

I text Fletcher.

Meet me in Carmen's room. I need your help.

I think it's OK to ask for help. I promised to be there for him. He promised to be there for me. If ever I needed someone to be there for me, it's now.

I sit on Carmen's bed and wait.

The bed has been stripped down to the mattress. A tower of clean sheets, pillowcases and new pillows is piled on one end. That means someone is moving in very soon. That means Fletcher and I will have to find somewhere else to meet.

My mind begins to spin. Where? We can't meet in Fletcher's room because of Lee. We can't meet in my room because boys aren't allowed in girls' rooms. Sexual relationships aren't allowed – one day at a time, none of you are ready for intimacy yet, Tony says. Anyway, we can't meet in either of those rooms because Carmen won't be there.

Carmen has to be there.

She started all this.

Only she knows the way out.

I sit on the bed and wait. I hold my knees up close to my chest and put my arms around them.

Oh, Carmen, please help. You understand.

Fletcher's taking ages. I don't mind. I just sit and rock myself forwards and backwards.

I don't know what to think. I don't know why I remembered that room. I'm not even sure it was *my* memory.

Was it somebody else's?

Maybe I imagined it. But can you imagine smells?

By the time Fletcher comes, I've rocked and rocked. I feel dizzy.

'What the hell's up with you?' asks Fletcher.

I want to tell him. I want to explain about going into that room and the smell and the body; how I was just trying because of him. And Carmen. How it's really his fault. But when I try, my throat feels so thin I can't even swallow. I can't get any words out. I just open and close my mouth, like I'm drowning in air.

'That serious?' says Fletcher.

I nod.

'Hell,' he says.

Tears well up in my eyes. My throat closes up. I flap my hand.

He gets it. That's one good thing about addicts. It's a special kind of club. Other addicts understand. You don't have to say much.

'OK,' says Fletcher. 'Nod your head for yes or shake your head for no. Raise your palm if it's too painful.'

I nod my head.

'Did you have a bad trip?' asks Fletcher.

I shake my head.

'Did you bug out in Circle Time?' He adds, 'Was it because Judith is such a dickhead?'

I shake my head. I hold my hand up. The tears brim so full they spill over on to my cheeks. I sniff. I drag the back of my sleeve across my eyes.

'So it's worse?' says Fletcher.

I nod. I wish I could tell him. My throat has fused shut.

'An early memory?'

I nod my head.

'Bad?'

I nod again. I make a sign with my hand in the air as if I'm turning a wheel.

'Worse than bad?'

I nod.

'Somebody beat you?'

I shake.

'Somebody touched you up?'

Shake.

'Somebody abused you full on?'

Shake.

'Were you in pain?'

Shake.

'I'm running out of ideas,' says Fletcher. 'Give me a clue.'

I get out my phone. I open up the notes. My fingers are shaking. I think I'm going to drop the phone. My hands. My palms. I'm sweating. I try to breathe. I type into the notes: *BODY*.

'There was a body?' says Fletcher. 'As in dead?'

I nod my head. I keep nodding. I drag my sleeve across my eyes again. My throat won't come unstuck. The Alien suddenly materializes, takes one look at me, shakes a dozen heads and spreads superglue across my lips. It blasts me with: 'We Must Not Tell Our Secrets.' It puts one of its tentacles under my chin and presses my lips firmly shut.

'You killed someone?' says Fletcher.

I shake my head.

'You watched while somebody killed someone?'

I shake my head. I don't think I did. I can't be sure. Maybe that's behind another locked door.

'So there's a random body somewhere in your past?'

The Alien is trying to superglue my eyes shut as well. I think I'm going to vomit. I don't know how I'll vomit if I can't open my mouth. I hope Fletcher gets to the truth soon. I'm so tired. I'll drown soon. I just want to roll into a small ball.

'Whose body was it?'

That's the thing. *I don't know.*

I don't know what I was doing in that room.

And I can't make it go away and it's freaking me out. IT'S FREAKING ME OUT.

'OK, OK,' says Fletcher. 'Breathe. Just breathe.'

I try, but I'm deep underwater.

'So you don't know what happened and you don't know who it was?' says Fletcher.

I nod.

'Well, I'm your recovery buddy,' says Fletcher, 'so I'll help you find out.'

The thought of going back into that room to find anything out is too much. I'm going to faint. I hold up my hand. I flap it. I rock on the bed.

Fletcher sits down beside me. He puts his lovely shoulders next to mine. He takes my hand in his, stops it flapping.

'It'll be a murder mystery, a whodunnit, a body in a locked room,' he says. 'It won't be scary at all. We'll be in it together the whole time. We'll be detectives. Don't worry. We'll find out everything. Maybe Judith's right even if she is a dickhead. Maybe we can undo all that shit. It will be OK.'

I don't say anything. The Alien has succeeded in supergluing my eyelids together. He's pressing on one of them with a tentacle. I help him. I press the knuckles of my left fist into the other eye socket.

Fletcher catches my fist, guides it down to my lap and holds it with my flapping hand.

'Hey, Dani, I'm here,' he says. 'I'm going to be here for you.'

And even though I can't see him, I know it's the real Fletcher sitting beside me now – not that goddamn awesome Detective Fletcher.

He puts his arm around my shoulders and hugs my Thinness to him.

I can't nod or shake my head or flap my hand or do anything any more.

'I'm just going to sit here,' he says. 'I'm just going to sit here, Dani, and hold you until you feel OK.'

11

Everybody runs strategies. Don't lie. Not to yourself. You're running a strategy right now. You probably repackage it and give it a nice name – like Kindness or Being Helpful – but you are running a shitty strategy and you know it.

Every strategy is about feeling good. Kindness and Being Helpful are just the same. The payoff is that you get to feel good about yourself. Your reward is doing Inner Talk that says: *I was kind to that person. I'm a good person. Because I'm a good person I'm allowed to feel good.*

I'm the Queen Of Strategies. I have a strategy for every second of every minute of every hour of every day. And I have back-up strategies should the original strategies fail.

Don't knock strategies. They're there when everybody else is not.

Right now I need my main strategy.

This is how it goes. It's quite simple. It runs on a point system. If I can get up to ten points in one day, then I'm allowed to feel good. But it's very tricky to get points. Here are some of the ways I can earn them.

First of all, I have to eat less than everybody else in the room. That means I must watch exactly how much everybody puts on their plate. I must watch every time anyone goes for a refill. I must decide who has the smallest plate of food in the room and I must make sure my portion is smaller.

If there's anyone in the room who eats nothing then I can't get the point. There's a strategy for that too – I'll tell you about it in a minute.

If I manage to eat less than everyone else at a set mealtime, I earn one point. But I automatically lose my point if someone leaves the room within ten minutes of eating because I can't rule out that they're bulimic. But I have a strategy for that as well.

All this means that I have to be present at every meal. I have to get there first and leave last. If I'm late to a mealtime then the best plan is not to eat at all.

Sometimes this strategy really works. Everybody arrives on time and everyone eats a lot of food. Then I can have something to eat *and* I can get the point too. That's ideal. But it's scary to commit to the food because if someone comes in late and decides not to eat anything, then I lose my point – in fact, I'm penalized for being too quick to stuff my face.

I can't regain the point even if I go to the toilet and puke everything up. In fact, I lose a point if I *don't* do that.

If I don't earn even one point in a day, it's just awful. I go around feeling that I'm the worst person in the world and totally unworthy of love.

I've never scored ten points in one day even though I've tried really hard. Before I came into recovery, I used to go into cafes and sit there for as long as possible, just to become a bit more lovable.

This Not Eating strategy comes with a health warning though.

Tony repeatedly advises me of the hazards of Not Eating. He calls them Dani's Toxic Problems Of The Heart.

He says because anorexics lose muscle mass, they lose heart muscle at a preferential rate. The heart becomes smaller and weaker so it gets worse at increasing circulation in response to exercise. Blood pressure drops and the pulse slows down.

This leads to chronic cardiac arrhythmia and delirium.

Otherwise known as heartbreak and madness.

Tony says both conditions can be fatal.

15

Fletcher is really serious about helping me. I've only ever seen his eyes light up like they're shining right now when he talks about crack. He says crack is awesome. It's the rest of the world that's shit. I guess that's part of his strategy. I don't disagree with him. I've never tried crack. I have tried the world.

'You're going to have to remember,' says Fletcher.

I shake my head. I'm not going back into that room.

'All the clues are there.' He leans forward and taps my forehead.

But he's right. Even Judith might be right. Though she must be running some kind of strategy too. Because it makes sense. Doesn't it? If you can unlock the past, find the thing that's damaged, yank it out and fix it, then you can recover.

'I know this is scary,' says Fletcher, 'but I'm here.'

How's that helpful? I roll my eyes at him.

Fletcher sighs. 'Being on the street teaches you things; the worst is that you're alone.'

It was the smell that was the worst.

'Being alone. Knowing that nobody will stop and help you. Nobody gives a shit. You're invisible. Unless you do something criminal. And that's a double bind. You get noticed, but in a bad way. It confirms the truth that you're not worth a goddamn thing.'

Oh God! Have I got to listen to his sob story now?

'So I'll give a shit,' says Fletcher. 'Here's the deal. I'll go first. I'll tell you the scariest thing I can remember about my past. Then you tell me the scariest thing about yours. Then it's my turn again. We'll keep going like that until we find something out.'

Yippee. I get his shit as well.

'That means you won't be alone. I'll be in the room with you and just as shit scared. Believe me, it helps if someone else is around. Plus this is Carmen's room, so she's here too. Sort of.'

My tongue is still stuck to the roof of my mouth. There's a hollow that runs from the back of my throat to the centre of my stomach. But what he's suggesting is a kind of strategy. Plus, I can lie.

I peel my tongue off the roof of my mouth. I try to make myself salivate. Just enough to croak out, 'Can we get points?'

Fletcher gives me a look.

'Maybe,' he says. 'But you don't get points for any old rubbish.'

So he knows about point systems.

'You only get a point if you make me goddamn cry out in horror,' he says. 'That's the deal. You can goddamn take it or goddamn leave it.'

I take it.

I need points badly.

56

16

'I'm going to tell you about my mum,' says Fletcher. 'But you mustn't think I didn't love her. That's the whole point of it. I did love her, but this is what she was like.'

'OK,' I whisper.

'She never approved of me. She said mean things in a very loving way. When they hurt me, she would deny that she'd said them on purpose. She'd say I was taking things the wrong way. That she only wanted to help me. But she never praised me – never said I'd done anything really well.'

'Maybe you didn't,' I say. God, this is so trivial.

'If I did achieve something – like I got good marks in a test, or I got chosen for the school team – she'd tell me how the son of a friend of hers had done something much better. Or she wouldn't say anything.'

Even the Alien yawns.

'But later on in the day she might say something very cruel, perhaps drag up something from the past that would embarrass the hell out of me, just to let me know I shouldn't think I was any kind of hot shit.'

At least he had a mum.

'She'd let me know that I was no good simply by comparison. She would wax on about how wonderful somebody else's kid was – how much she would have loved to be the mother of that kid. She could tell me what rubbish I was by not even saying a word.'

The Alien actually falls asleep.

'She could bring me down when I was totally happy just by the tone of her voice. You can't confront a tone of voice. When you're a little kid you don't even know why you've suddenly changed from being very happy to very miserable.'

'OK, my turn,' I croak out.

'And when I began to understand it, I couldn't challenge it because she totally denied it.'

I should learn to be more patient.

'I learned to be afraid of telling her anything. Afraid of smiling, afraid of being happy. As a result I was always afraid and always in the wrong, and I could never put my finger on it. Sometimes her tone of voice was accompanied by a particular glance, locking her eye on me. When she just glanced in that way, my heartbeat would shoot up and I'd break out in a cold sweat and start to stutter.'

Actually, it sounds horrible.

'And it meant I was alone. Completely alone. I didn't have any brothers or sisters. There was nobody I could tell. And even if there was somebody, I didn't have the language to explain that look in her eye, how it drilled down into me and hollowed me out, until I was all empty inside. So I lived like that. And I loved her. And I accepted that I was to blame. I didn't dare tell anyone about her drinking. She said it was my fault she had to drink so much. And I said sorry.'

OK, my turn.

'In public she would always act really concerned. She'd make sure that I could overhear it when she said, "I feel sorry for Fletcher. He's so sensitive. He doesn't seem to know who he is. And he has such a bad time. He has absolutely no friends – nobody likes him at all. I've tried to tell him he needs to be nicer and less selfish and impatient. He should be more helpful and generous and have fun, for God's sake! He needs to lighten up! Nobody likes boring, depressing people. I don't know how I can get that message across to him."'

OK, not my turn.

'She was right about me not knowing who I am. Back then it was worse. I was a total confused mess. Once I did try to talk to someone, a counsellor at school. They called my mum in. It was the worst thing I ever did. At home I was made to suffer for that for a very long time. And at school, the counsellor told me that my mother talked about me in the most caring way, and that perhaps I had got things wrong because I was so sensitive and maybe just a teeny-weeny bit selfish.'

I've heard enough.

'Ana is my best friend,' I say.

'Who's Anna?' asks Fletcher.

I look at Fletcher. Unbelievable. I'm prepared to share my worst secret and apparently he's never heard of Ana! I'm not going to discuss her identity. Any anorexic can tell you about

Ana. If he's so unaware, it's not my job to educate him. So I just carry on.

'Ana makes the good times better and the hard times easier,' I say.

I'm being so very fake. I'm almost sorry for him. No wonder his mum gave him the runaround for so long. I know I have to do better. I know I'm supposed to share my most feared memory right now. Instead I share some thinspirational tips.

'Ana helps me to distract myself from food,' I say. 'She tells me to keep myself busy all day with things to stop me thinking about eating. She told me not to eat my sadness. If I'm feeling sad or crap I must listen to music or do some activity. I must never eat when I'm unhappy.'

'You never eat at all,' points out Fletcher.

'She told me to write words like "bovine" and "deformed" with a Sharpie on my stomach to remind me that Fat Is Ugly. She told me never to eat when I'm distracted or doing something else. She taught me never to eat after seven P.M. or before seven A.M. She told me if you drink water in between each bite of food it fills you up quicker. Iced water, obviously. She told me never to eat alone. And to do thinspo.'

'Thinspo?' asks Fletcher.

'It's just a collection of inspirations, like pictures,' I say. 'I keep mine on my phone. Any time I feel my resolve weaken, I look at my thinspo collection.'

'What are they pictures of?' asks Fletcher.

'Of thin people, obviously,' I say.

'How is this a bad memory?' says Fletcher.

For one horrible minute I think he's going to ask me if I'll show him my collection of thinspo. And he has noticed I'm not sharing. The moment passes. My Thinness is safe. I shouldn't have taken this route. Now I'm stuck.

'You can use a reward system too. Every time you want to eat something and you overcome the desire, you can reward yourself with a one-pound coin in your special Thinness piggy bank.'

'Dani, we're supposed to be working on our recovery, not boasting about our addictions.'

'And there are rubber bands and aphorisms to overcome cravings. I can give myself three smart pings on the wrist, so that it really hurts, and say to myself sixty times, "I don't want to eat. I don't want to eat. I don't want to eat." That usually works.'

'That sounds messed up,' says Fletcher.

I shrug.

'And you haven't actually told me *anything* about your worst experience,' says Fletcher.

'I've told you about my problem,' I say. 'That is my worst experience.' I put on my Circle Time voice. 'My name is Dani, and I am an anorexic.'

'I know, Dani,' says Fletcher, 'but you've got to do better. This hasn't given me anything to go on. We're trying to solve a whodunnit. Tell me about your first foster placement – anything you remember.'

'My first foster placement was with a family that lived in a big house,' I say. 'They fostered loads of kids. That was their job – their income. That's how they kept themselves going,

61

fostering kids like me. There were up to five of us fostered kids plus their three real kids. It wasn't very nice. We always had to catch the 171 bus to get anywhere and we could never sit together. There just wasn't enough space – I remember that. At mealtimes there was a two-sitting system because the dining room had been converted into an extra bedroom, and the kitchen was too small for everyone to fit in. Their kids sat down first. We had to wait in the front room until we were called in for the leftovers. Sometimes they'd scrape the remains off their plates on to ours.'

Fletcher looks sad. 'How old were you?'

'I was seven.'

I was quite old enough to know what was going on.

17

Three loud bangs on my door. I wake up. It's dark.

'Open up,' says a voice.

It's the middle of the night.

For a minute I think it's Fletcher. He's come to put his arms around me. He's going to hold me. He's going to let me rest my head on his lovely shoulders. I'm surprised at how much I'd like that.

'Open up,' says the voice again. It's Tony.

I open up.

'Surprise search,' says Tony. 'Just sit on the chair by the window.'

I sit down on the chair by the window. I've only got a T-shirt on and boy boxers. I shiver. An irrational fear that Tony is going to touch me pops into my head.

Tony wedges the door open. Two of the care workers come in. They turn on all the lights.

Why did I think that? About being molested? Something deep inside my memory goes click.

It's so cold with the door open.

They systematically search my room.

'What are you looking for?' I ask, as one of them tips my clothes out of a drawer.

'The usual,' says Tony.

A pair of knickers lands by his foot.

'I'm anorexic,' I say. 'You won't find anything in here.'

'You'd be surprised,' says Tony.

I am surprised.

'Why this late?' I ask.

Tony fixes me with a look. 'You know the rules,' he says.

For some reason one of the rehab rules states that counsellors don't have to disclose why they do what they do. Unlike us addicts. We have to disclose not only why we do what we do, but why we don't do what we don't do. Not to mention why we think what we should not.

'Has something happened?' I ask.

Tony tips my washbag out on the bed.

'Is it Fletcher?' A sudden panic seizes me.

'We're done.' Tony quickly shoves my belongings back into my locker. He nods at the care workers as if to say: Let's move on to the next.

One drawer tips open. A bunch of my stuff falls on the floor.

'Pick that up,' Tony says to one of the workers. He leaves.

'What happened?' I ask her. She's not a proper care worker. She used to be one of us state-funded addicts, but she did so well at recovery she landed herself a job. She bends down to scoop up a sports top. I know her slightly. I think she 'diets' too.

'Drugs,' she mutters.

I get it. Somebody has brought some stuff in and is dealing. This is how the centre goes about finding out who's involved. They could have just asked, but that would've been too simple. Plus being questioned about old sly habits might trigger our addictions. Plus we're all liars. Better to jump a surprise search on everyone.

'What will happen when they catch them?' I ask.

The girl draws a finger across her throat. She twists an imaginary noose tight; her mouth slops open into a silly hideous grin. She strings herself up. She whispers, 'Death by dismissal,' in a conspiratorial way, then leaves.

I get back into bed. I'm so cold. A silly hideous grin. I'm shivering. A noose around a neck. A man coming into a room. I want to text Fletcher. I'm praying it's not him picking up drugs again. He said he was barely hanging on. If he's using again and they throw him out I don't know what I'll do. Carmen was hanging on. A man in a room abusing me. I reach for my phone. I need him. I pick it up. No, Carmen was just hanging. We have a deal. He can't get thrown out.

There are two messages.

The Circle Alert:
Something is up. Watch out. Surprise search. If you're hiding any gear, stash it in pre-planned hiding place or dispose.

I flick to the second message.
A voicemail from Fletch:

'Might be a good idea to hide your phone. If they see your thinspo, it won't look good.

'Anyway, I've been working on the case. Here's a round-up of my notes. I'll read them out for you.

'Findings so far:

'Dani put in care at four? Six?

'Dani put with various foster families at seven.

'Dani thinks she was in Lewisham area.

'There was a no. 171 bus.

'The 171 goes through Lewisham. Checked.

'OK, now, things to find out:

'Location of the locked room.

'What school did you go to? (It's likely that foster place-ment would be in the area of school.)

'Can you ask someone to go into Lewisham Borough Council (fostering services or similar?) to see if they have any records of your placements? (No point calling – I tried. You just get automated voices shit.)

'Get back to me with everything you remember about school or anything.

'I'm so glad you're my recovery buddy. It felt so good tell-ing you about my mum. For the first time I didn't feel disloyal. I didn't feel scared. It felt good. I'm putting my arms around you and holding you tight, Dani. Metaphorically obviously. We'll get to the bottom of all this. Absolutely. Thank you for being my friend.

'Sleep tight.'

I put the phone under my pillow. For some silly reason, I lay my cheek over it and hug the pillow.

Room Empty

I usually hug my Thinness.
I will try to always be kind to Fletcher.
I could message Kerstin about Lewisham Social Services.
I will not think about the locked room.
I will not think about the locked room.
I will not think about the locked room.
I will not think about the locked room.

18

In the morning I make it to Circle Time. I just sit there. Sometimes the pressure to contribute to the discussion and share your stuff is bad. I can't share anything today. Even talking is hard.

I didn't bother going down to breakfast. I didn't even bother trying to score a point. Breakfast is usually easy because I'm not very hungry in the mornings.

'Hi, I'm Judith, and I'm your psychodynamic counsellor.'

'Hi, Judith,' we say, all interested like she has never told us this before.

'Today we're going to revisit Step One of our twelve-step recovery programme,' says Judith. 'After any major setback – after our closure yesterday, and the disruption – it's a good idea to revisit the journey we've taken so far.'

I wonder why she can't actually say Carmen's name. Now Carmen has become 'closure', 'a major setback', an impediment to our recovery. It really sucks to be dead.

And I'm a 'disruption'.

'So I'm going to remind us of our first principle, namely that we admitted that we were powerless and our lives had become unmanageable. Before we begin sharing, let's do some focused thinking,' says Judith. She smiles at all of us, beams down from a great height. 'Would anyone like to discuss why the first step is written in the past tense?'

There's a silence. None of us raises our hand. That's not because we don't have answers. It's because we don't raise hands in recovery. That would be admitting that we need permission to speak. And we cannot admit that. Because as freethinking, recovering young adults, we don't need to ask for permission to be ourselves. Which is complete crap. We need permission to do everything here.

But we all play the game. We sit back in our chairs, contemplating our strategies. I've already got one point today for skipping breakfast.

Lee can't focus very well this morning. His pupils are suspiciously dilated. He has a silly grin all over his face.

'Hi, I'm Cormac. I'm an addict.' At last, someone plays ball. Cormac (that's Iggy) runs a hand through his mop of reddish hair.

'Hi Cormac/Iggy,' everyone answers.

'I think Step One is written in the past tense because we're all on our road to recovery now,' says Cormac. He grins at us across the circle. He knows he's just spoken complete bollocks. One look at me is enough to realize that not everybody is on the road to recovery.

Lee spreads the grin wider. Step One can be written in whatever tense it wants. It has nothing to do with him.

'A very interesting response,' says Judith. 'And I think on the whole I agree with you. The past tense is a definite reminder that we're not powerless over our own addictions any more. We're not powerless and we can create our own preferred futures.'

Fletcher looks like he wants to be sick.

Judith continues, 'And the fact that it's written in the plural means that we have support and companions as we move forward along our path to recovery. I'd like you all to take a minute to close your eyes and visualize the pathway to recovery, leading uphill to a glorious summit where the Whole Picture will be spread before you, and from this elevated position you can see your way clearly.'

Fletcher is definitely going to be sick.

'And now we come to the paradox inside the first step,' says Judith. 'The paradox of powerlessness, in which we must surrender in order to win.'

I can see she'll soon be intoxicated with her own insight.

I look at the clock. Another three quarters of an hour until coffee break. I'm allowed coffee. Black, obviously. But I imagine putting milk in it. I imagine ladling heaped sugars into it. I think about the way I could lick the spoon after, even if I don't drink it.

'We're powerless because our addictions have caused us to have a compulsion and an obsession,' says Judith. She smiles around at all of us. 'Would anyone here like to explain the difference between compulsion and obsession?'

Lee grins and laughs, then raises his hand.

'There's no need to raise your hand, Lee,' says Judith. 'We're in recovery, we're on our paths together and we don't need permission to be ourselves.'

Lee doesn't take any notice. He waves and waves his hand like a little kid in the front row, eager to answer the question.

'Yes, Lee,' says Judith, with a pained look stretching across her mouth.

'A compulsion is when you just have to do something even though you don't want to, like if you wanna get stoned and you just have to get stoned.' He giggles. 'You do it even if you know you're not supposed to, like in the rules of rehab or if your mum tells you not to. You don't take no notice of them, and, like, yeah, so you just keep on, like, getting stoned.'

Looks like Lee has got a good understanding of the word 'compulsion'.

'And obsession?' asks Judith.

Lee is waving his hand again and almost falling off his chair. It looks like he's about to get the giggles properly.

'An obsession is when you, like, keep thinking about getting stoned and shit,' he shouts out. 'Because you want to do it and you keep thinking about it, and the thoughts go around and around and around and then some more, and every time you do it you keep thinking about doing it again.'

'Yes,' says Judith coldly. 'When you share, you need to remember to acknowledge your recovery and communicate your name.'

'Hi, MY NAME IS LEE,' shouts Lee. 'I am an ADDICT!'

This is becoming fun.

'Hi, Lee!' everyone shouts back.

Lee is about to say something pretty stupid.

Fletcher cuts into the slight pause he leaves.

'Hi, my name is Fletcher. I am an addict.'

Everyone sighs.

Everyone knows that Fletcher is rescuing Lee. Everyone wishes Fletcher would stop it and let Lee have his say. Everyone knows that Fletcher cannot save Lee. Everyone except Fletcher.

'OK, so powerlessness means that you have no control over your addiction,' says Fletcher. 'It means that you recognize that it's in control and you're not. And it's kind of like . . .' He pauses. 'Let's say somebody told you they'd give you a million pounds if you jumped out of an aeroplane with no parachute. I'd say no, because I don't have control over gravity so I wouldn't survive. I'm powerless against it. So you have to admit that you're powerless over your addiction and that it will kill you. You have to be convinced of it and afraid in the same way of jumping without a parachute. That's what I think about powerlessness.'

I'd like to clap for Fletcher. He's trying so hard to recover. He's trying way harder than anyone else in the room. But he's probably the least likely to succeed, because he's only trying hard to please Judith. And maybe to please me a little bit; maybe to please everybody else too. Who knows. But he's not trying really hard to please Fletcher.

He admitted to me last night he doesn't even know who Fletcher is.

At coffee break, I ask Fletcher, 'What was up last night?'

Fletcher rolls his eyes, nods towards Judith and Tony. They're standing by the wall watching.

Nuff said.

I help myself to a cup of black coffee. I don't consider the biscuits, but I look longingly at the milk and sugar.

Fletcher grabs a fig roll. He whispers, 'They kicked Alice out.'

'What?'

I'm actually shocked.

Alice was such a quiet, nervous, timid thing. In fact, she was the kind of person who made a room feel emptier when she was in it.

'Shush,' says Fletcher.

'But what for?' I ask.

'Apparently she was cutting herself and then overdosing on prescription painkillers.'

'But where's she gone?' I ask.

'Who knows?' whispers Fletcher. 'The place where they all disappear to.'

I send him an 'Uh?'

'The real world.'

The real world, like Outer Space. Cold and dark and endless. A place where you're bound to get sucked into a bottomless black hole. And be lost for ever. Poor Alice.

In recovery they skate over the problem of reality. They just tell you you need to deal with life on life's terms.

Life's terms: just Alice and her Stanley knife and a packet of codeine.

She was only fourteen.

'It was Carmen,' says Fletcher.

'What?' I say again.

'Didn't you know?' says Fletcher. 'Alice had a thing about Carmen.'

I didn't know.

I feel sorry for Alice.

That's what they don't tell you in recovery about life's terms . . .

Reality is shit.

19

'C'mon,' says Fletcher. 'Let's get out of here and do a Sherlock.'

I turn the corners of my mouth down.

'Let's just do it,' says Fletcher.

I raise one shoulder and let it fall.

'You know something about you, Dani?' he says. 'You're a miserable git. Trust me for half an hour, OK?'

I'm not sure I trust him, but half an hour isn't too long.

Together we climb the stairs. I lean on Fletcher. He half carries me. It must be nice to have strong shoulders. The library is on the fifth floor. Books. Computer hubs. The ceiling is slanted and vast. Planked floors run the length of the building.

'I love coming up here,' he says.

We settle down on one of the benches. Fletcher turns on the computer and we start searching. Well, Fletcher does. He searches the County Court records in Lewisham.

Fletcher is always trying to do things for others. It

could get on your nerves if you hadn't made a conscious decision to trust him. Right now he's trying a bit too hard though.

'After the search, I lay there in the middle of the night,' he says, 'and it suddenly struck me that if you were put in care there must be some kind of a legal document on it.'

He's right, of course.

'It would be registered in the court's archives.'

I lean forward. I peer into the screen.

'If I can just find out which court.'

The sides of our heads touch.

'They store all their records online.'

I push his face out of the way.

'How can I see anything with your fat head there?' I say.

Fletcher tries to manoeuvre back in. 'I think there's enough space to share.'

I make a disgruntled noise.

After a second, Fletcher backs away.

'There you go,' he says. 'Not because I have X-ray vision, but because I'm the bigger person. You have the screen.'

I ignore him. I hog all the space. It's not much fun. I don't really know what I'm looking for.

After a minute, I say, 'I don't mind sharing the screen with you, as long as you promise you don't have head lice.'

'I do not have head lice,' says Fletcher very solemnly.

'All addicts have head lice,' I say.

He giggles.

'Head lice and crabs and body lice and scabies.'

He does exaggerated, junkie-style, crawling-skin scratching.

For some reason we both find that hysterically funny. I start laughing. Fletcher itches up and down his scalp.

Jennifer, on a computer at the far end of the library, says, 'Shush.'

That makes it worse. Fletcher points at Jennifer and does total body rash.

I swallow laughter. It comes gurgling back out. It explodes in a great shower.

'Ugh,' says Fletcher, 'you just spat on my cheek.'

'Sorry,' I say in between each spraying. 'Sorry.'

I'm holding the laughter in so hard my ribs crack. My chest shoots out all over the computer screen. My sides split and the laughter escapes in clouds.

'Sorry,' I wheeze. My eyes melt and trickle down the sides of my face.

'I don't mind,' he says. 'You're beautiful when you laugh, Dani.'

I gulp and swallow.

'But it's distracting,' he says. 'And I can't be Sherlock Holmes properly with spit all over me. So stop laughing and go back to being miserable.'

And that makes me laugh even more.

Fletcher takes out a tissue and wipes the shower of saliva off his cheek. I don't dare to say sorry a third time or I'll explode into a million droplets.

Fletcher sends out a look that is all safety net and feather down. It catches my eye and dissolves.

And, in that moment, the library holds its breath.

Fletcher is my friend. My very own friend, who I can shower with laughter. It's so good to laugh. I want to laugh with him for ever. I raise my finger and wipe away a tear from my cheek.

I promise myself to always laugh with Fletcher, for ever and for ever. I rub another tear away.

Fletcher catches my hand and guides my damp finger to his lips.

The universe comes to a stop.

He presses my finger dry.

Jennifer looks over and frowns.

The screen in front of us scrolls down through endless convictions.

Family Court records.

Abusive relationships.

Children put in care.

Custody cross-petitions.

Click. A tiny box locked in another tiny box, locked somewhere in that empty room, in the deep recesses of my brain, clicks and clicks again. Abusive relationships.

I draw in a breath.

Fletcher notices immediately. 'What is it? Tell me which case? Do they look familiar? Do you recognize a name? Dani?'

His questions wash the click away.

'It's nothing,' I say.

I don't want it to be anything. But now I've thought of it, I can't seem to stop it itching. Deep down. Scratch, scratch. An abusive relationship. A man enters. An empty room. *Click. Click.* In the box.

20

After break, during the second half of Circle Time, we have to continue sharing about powerlessness.

'Hi, I'm Verity,' says Verity. 'And I'm an addict.'

Obviously coffee has revived Verity.

'Hello, Verity,' we all chime.

'Powerlessness means that you have no idea how to stop once you start. I mean, once you start indulging in your addiction. And you have no idea what place you might end up in either – you could do a line of coke on a Saturday morning and by Sunday be dead. That's all.'

Thanks, Verity.

Atticus decides to join in. 'Hi, I'm Atticus. I'm an addict.'

'Hi, Atticus.'

The power of coffee is impressive. I'm pretty sure if it wasn't needed to get people talking it would be a banned substance at DBRC.

'To me, powerless means stupidity,' says Atticus. 'If you keep on doing something like throwing yourself against a wall and every time you do it you get bruises and you end up bleeding, then sooner or later you have to realize you should stop throwing yourself against the wall, because when you do you're powerless to stop the bruising and bleeding.'

Atticus looks like he might add to that. Perhaps he'll entertain us with how he's powerless to stop himself smelling if he doesn't wash, or burping if he has gas.

Judith comes to the rescue. 'Thank you,' she says with a well-timed smile. 'Your contributions have been very thought-provoking. I think for the remainder of our session we should break out and revisit our inventory of all the negative side effects caused by our powerlessness over our addictions and compulsions. We need to revisit the ways in which our lives are unmanageable.'

Oh joy.

She hands out our folders.

We find our recovery buddies. We flip down desktops from the sides of the chairs. We pull out our inventories. I read through mine.

DANI'S INVENTORY OF CATASTROPHIC SIDE EFFECTS
- extreme weight loss
- thin appearance
- abnormal blood cell counts
- elevated liver enzymes
- fatigue
- dizziness and fainting
- seizures

- *brittle nails*
- *delirium*

'I don't think much of your list,' says Fletcher.

'Well, there are more points on mine than yours,' I say.

'I don't think that "a thin appearance" counts as a negative side effect for you.'

'It's still a negative side effect though.'

'You're being defensive,' says Fletcher. 'You're supposed to write down things like "being unable to pass my exams because I was too tired to revise" or "being unable to go out with my friends because they're going to a restaurant. So, no friendships." That sort of thing. Things which affect you personally. Not some biological list.'

I grab his list.

'Well, I don't think much of yours either. What does "no money" and "no possessions" and "lost everything" mean? Who ever heard of a crack addict with a television?'

We're interrupted by Judith. Perhaps she overheard us.

'Try to include detailed examples of what your addictions have done to you mentally, physically, spiritually, financially, socially and legally,' she says. 'And ask yourself: Am I hiding anything? Secrecy is always an indication of unmanage-ability.'

Lee giggles.

Everybody looks at Lee. It's embarrassing.

Lee turns towards Judith. 'You're right, boss,' he says.

She narrows her eyes. 'If you truly accept the premise of this first step – that you're genuinely powerless and that your lives have become unmanageable – I don't think any of you would return to your addictions.'

I notice she has subtly changed the pronoun of the first step.

STEP FOUR
SEARCHING AND FEARLESS

21

During one-to-one counselling, my mobile vibrates. When I have a chance, I slide it out.

It's a text from Fletcher: *Meet me in Carmen's room tonight.*

So I do.

We don't put on the light. The staff might see it and find us out of bed.

Fletcher has brought a laptop with him. We're not allowed laptops or video games or handheld playthings. We're not really allowed mobiles. But Tony has turned a blind eye to mobiles. That's because he relies on his mobile. He needs it so that he can slip out and have a fag any time he wants and text another counsellor to cover for him. It's his personal strategy. It's called If I Let You Get Away With It, You Have To Let Me Get Away With It Too.

But laptops are different.

'Wow,' I say. 'Where did you get *that*?'

'Lee,' says Fletcher. 'He's got about ten of them stashed under his bed.'

I don't need to ask why. Everybody runs a strategy, don't they?

'They nearly found them last night,' says Fletcher.

We're supposed to be developing hobbies in recovery. Things that engage and inspire us. I guess nobody told Lee that stealing should not be one of them.

'How did he manage to hide ten laptops?' I ask.

'Bagged them up, leaned out of the window and slung them from the drainpipe.'

'Blimey.'

'I thought the plastic would rip and they'd crash down.'

'Wasn't a very thorough search then,' I say. 'Tony should have known to check outside windows.'

'Lucky for us.'

'Tony likes you, that's why.'

'Now we can continue with The Mystery Of The Body In The Locked Room,' says Fletcher, patting the laptop.

I wince.

'Let's get back to the location where all this happened – the scene of the crime type thing. Where do you actually come from? And where do you think the Locked Room is?' says Fletcher, all Sherlock plus Poirot. 'Search outwards from a given point. Use all available clues. Might be easier than searching court records. Are we still thinking Lewisham?'

'Maybe,' I say. 'Or New Cross.'

'Why?' Fletcher's fingers are poised above the keyboard.

I shrug.

I don't know. That's just what I think.

'OK,' says Fletcher, 'let's make it Lewisham/New Cross.'

He does a quick search on Google, typing in my name, 'dead body', 'locked room', 'Lewisham' and 'New Cross'.

'We can't meet here any more,' I say.

'We can always use the library,' says Fletcher. 'Which school did you go to?'

'Deptford Park.'

'And what do you remember of your family before you were put into care?'

My Alien jumps straight out to defend me. Before Fletcher realizes anything, the Alien's got tentacles wound all around his neck and is stringing him up towards the ceiling. Fletcher has this look of surprise on his face.

'Hey!' Fletcher croaks. 'Don't jump down my throat.'

I call the Alien to order. I put it on a leash. I tie it to the leg of the bed.

'Sorry,' I manage. 'I didn't mean to snap at you.'

'Yell, scream and swear,' corrects Fletcher.

The Alien squirms. Its suckers turn yellow and start to ooze mucus.

'Rewind,' I say. 'We can't meet here anymore. Because Carmen is dead and somebody new is going to be in this room tomorrow.'

'What was all that about?' says Fletcher.

'All what?' I ask.

'Knock it off, Dani,' says Fletcher. 'I'm trying to help you.'

I don't want him to help me and I can't tell him anything about my life before I went into care. I don't remember it.

Fletcher Googles all the care homes around Lewisham where a six-year-old girl might have been put. He gets lost on the

Sarah Mussi

council website and ends up on a page about recycling rubbish. He rearranges words in the search box and tries again.

'I'm not sure this research is going to work either,' says Fletcher at last. 'I need a bit more to go on. I've tried typing your name into the search, but it's not coming up with anything to do with Dani Spencer.'

'I wasn't Dani Spencer then,' I say.

'Whaa?'

'They changed my name,' I say.

'Who changed your name?'

'I don't know. The social workers or care officers – the adults in charge of me, I guess.'

'Why did they do that?'

'If I knew, we wouldn't need all this research,' I say.

Fletcher sighs, like: You could have said so before. 'OK, so what was your original name?'

This time I manage to hold on to the chain before the Alien completely flattens Fletcher. The chain is very slippery because the Alien has been secreting a nasty, thick, sticky, sludgy slime all over the floor. I know it won't take much more of this prying. I notice my fingers are trembling as I grip the chain. I notice my chest is hollow and unreasonable. My heart fumbles. I'm going to have to tell Fletcher to back off.

'I don't know my name from before.'

It's all been wiped out. I don't know who my mum was. I don't know where I came from.

I close my eyes and see the doorway that Judith built in my mind. There's a shadow across it. I'm not going to open that door ever again. I'll work my strategies. I'll be OK.

'Just leave it,' I say, opening my eyes.

Fletcher looks fed up. 'I wish you'd let me help you,' he says. 'You do this on purpose, don't you? You need to stop it. You need to start allowing people to help you.'

I don't know why he's wasting his time. Nobody has ever done anything for me before. Does he think if someone starts caring now, it's going to wipe out seventeen years of nothing? If so, he's hilarious.

'You don't want to get well, do you?' says Fletcher. 'You're just like Lee.'

You're waking up. Yes, Fletcher, I am just like Lee. He doesn't want to give up his addiction and neither do I. No addict ever wants to stop. If we could magic away all the bad stuff, we'd be perfectly happy. Take Carmen, for example – she seemed so sorted, but when the time came to live the dream, she hanged herself with an old scarf and shat all down her leg. That's how much she loved her future sober life.

The Alien stops emitting slime and shakes out its tentacles. It shakes and shakes, until it looks like a little furry teddy bear.

Fletcher looks at me sadly.

'I will help you,' he says, 'whether you want me to or not.'

22

We can't meet in Carmen's room any more. The new girl has moved in. Her name is Alice Munro.

Another Alice. What is it with that name?

I don't know what her choice addiction is. I should knock on Carmen's door and say hello but I don't really feel strong enough. Plus it would involve talking and all that.

I get a text from Fletcher. *In a bad way. Need help.*

So now it's him?

Maybe he's forgotten I'm the one in a bad way. I'm the one who needs the help. I told him to stop pouring himself into me. Now look where it's got him.

This is exactly what addicts do to each other.

I text him back. *I'm in a worse way. I'm drowning.*

I did warn him. Addicts are bad news. No boundaries. Judith says it's boundaries that keep us safe.

I get a reply before I've barely sent mine.

He writes, *I need fresh air. I need to get away from this place. If I don't, I think I'm going to quit.*

A hole opens up somewhere in the backyard of the universe. I can feel it sucking me in.

I text him back: *Try to hang on. It can't get much worse.*

Then I add: *Think of your Higher Power; believe in it. Maybe pray to it, like Tony says. Even if it's crack. Let's meet in the garden.*

I don't know why I suggest that. I'll have to go all the way down the back staircase. Every time I do that, I meet Carmen. Then I can't stop thinking of her. Not that I mind thinking of Carmen. I think of her pretty much all the time anyway. It helps to stop me thinking about food and the body in the locked room. Her body wasn't in any room. But I'll have to go past the kitchen and the smell of food sometimes makes me faint. Maybe that's why I suggested it.

Whatever, I rationalize. Conditional love is better than no love. A deal is a deal. Recovery buddies until the end.

So there is an end?

Oh, God.

I realize how final all this is.

I text Fletcher again: *Right at the bottom of the garden, down by the wall, where the little seat is.*

Nobody goes there. The garden bench has broken planking. The gardener dumps the grass cuttings in a pile right beside it. The whole area is overgrown with climbers and stuff.

I wind a scarf around my neck. I pull my jacket on. It's still spring, but I'm cold all the time. Sometimes even a hot bath fails to warm me up.

I leave my room. I pass Carmen's old one. Alice is lying on the bed. Maybe she's sleeping. She's very quiet.

I seem to be moving very slowly. I hold on to the walls. It's two days now since I ate anything. I got points though.

In my mind I get to the back staircase. I see Carmen's shadow hanging over the stairwell. It takes longer to get there in reality.

I take hold of the banister and focus on each step. 'This is no way to live your life,' says Carmen. 'You came here hoping to recover.' She sounds very disappointed.

She doesn't understand. I never wanted to leave my Thinness. I just wanted to cheat death.

I stop and ask Carmen, 'So why? Why didn't you want to cheat death?'

She laughs. 'Death was just the last barrier I had to remove from my recovery,' she says.

I think about that.

The flame inside me that wants to stay alive is very small. I could curl up in Outer Space. Even a little puff could blow it out. I could spin off into the outer darkness for ever.

'I hope you're free now,' I whisper.

I pause at the bottom of the stairwell. The smell is over-powering. I take the last step. They're frying fish and chips. I hang on to the banister more tightly. Such heady perfume. I breathe it in and let it fill my lungs. Today is Friday. You can do that, you know. It's a sub-strategy.

This is how it goes: when I'm very hungry and I smell something delicious, I just inhale. I tell myself I'm allowed to do that. Smell has no calories. I can enjoy it. It doesn't mean I have to eat anything.

And that's what I do. I stand there, balanced on the last

step, breathing in eau de fish and chips as if it were the perfume of the gods.

When at last the scent fades, I move on. That happens – things lose their magic if you over-smell them. You try it. Pick up a flower and breathe it in, like a rose or something. The first rush is exotic, intoxicating. The second sniff is pretty good, but by the time you've got to the tenth inhalation, you can't smell rose or fish and chips or anything any more.

Outside, I go down the steps at the back of the house. It's an average kind of day. The sun isn't shining, but it's not raining either.

My third day of not eating.

There's nobody in the garden. The gardener hasn't cut the grass. Dew soaks into my trainers. I could take the path. It's all paved in reconstituted stone. I feel very dizzy. Suddenly the gateway to the beyond at the crematorium flashes into my mind. Fake Cotswold paving. Waiting to welcome me.

I don't walk on the path. That would be too easy. If I was the kind of person who walked along paths I wouldn't be here.

I repeat to myself three times:

I won't die today.

I won't die today.

I won't die today.

Tony says neurolinguistic programming doesn't work if you say it in the negative.

I correct myself.

I will live today.

I will live today.
I will live today.

I like to feel the softness of the earth beneath my trainers. That's because the mind is forced to think about the thing it doesn't want to happen. And focusing on it makes it more likely to happen. Halfway down the garden are a few more steps. There are no railings here to hang on to, so very carefully I balance and take each step one at a time.

It's a paradox.

A bit like life.

I make it to where the rose beds are. I walk between them and down to the very bottom of the garden, where they throw the rubbish. I see the bust-up bench. I like that bench. I can identify with it. Put out here, in all winds and weather, broken but not quite discarded yet.

I make it to the bench. I sit down on its disintegrating slats and stare at the pile of grass cuttings in front of me.

A blackbird sings high up on the wall, there in the rambling honeysuckle. It lets out such sweet notes. I think, *Life could be beautiful.*

Fletcher arrives. He was right. He's in a bad way. You can tell when someone is in a bad way. There's some kind of line across their face, a twist of the mouth and a certain colouring. In fact, if I didn't know Fletcher pretty well, I don't think I'd recognize him. He's chain smoking roll-ups. He doesn't sit down on the bench. He's very agitated. He jumps straight up again. He paces about. He pulls at leaves and breaks twigs off.

'I just don't know what to do,' he mutters.

I don't say anything. I'm having a hard enough time trying not to topple off the seat I'm shivering so violently.

'Look at you,' Fletcher says.

'I can't look at me because I'm me and I don't have a mirror.'

'Stop it!' Fletcher yells.

'Stop what?' I say. Even at the eleventh hour, I can't stop it. Even though I know I'm killing us.

Fletcher straightens up. He takes a deep breath. He forces himself to stop pacing around. He shreds leaves with his fingers.

'OK,' he says, 'so it's like that, is it? OK. Shall we try to do some positive stuff?'

'OK,' I say.

'We did sharing our worst fears,' says Fletcher. 'Now let's share our happiest memory. Let's try to think of something worth living for.'

'OK,' I say. I must try.

'You start,' he says. 'I always do the talking.'

'My happiest memory?' I say.

'Yes.'

'My happiest memory,' I say, 'was when I was eleven. At the home, we had a day out, and our regular care worker was ill so we had a supply care worker from some agency or other. She was much older than the others, maybe in her sixties. We all went to the sea for the day. It was somewhere in Essex and the whole place smelled sugary, of toffee apples and candy-floss.' I pause. I take a deep breath. 'Yes, and savoury – it smelled of burgers and hot dogs and frying onions and raw sea salt. And we walked along the beach. And she let us have whatever we wanted. That day I ate Dunkin' Donuts, a Mr Whippy ice cream, scampi and chips.

'We sat on the pier and tried to skim pebbles. You can't really skim pebbles in the sea because of the waves and we were too high up, but it didn't matter.' I take a breath. I can almost feel the sun on my back. 'And Maggie, the supply care worker, was in a good mood all day, and she put her arm around me and told me I was a great kid. And the sun shone, and the afternoon lasted for ever. That was the best day of my life.'

I close my eyes as I think of that day. I can still feel the heat on my skin and smell the frying onions.

'Your turn,' I say.

Fletcher looks at me. His eyes are wide. 'My best day?' He stops.

'Go on,' I say.

'My best day was when you agreed to be there for me,' he says.

I raise my eyebrows. 'I thought we were doing historical best days?'

'There were no historical best days,' he says.

I stop shivering. 'I don't know what that means.'

'Everything up until the time I met you was shit,' says Fletcher. 'That's all. That's all it means.'

A strange fluttering starts at the nape of my neck. It spreads across my ribcage.

I want to hear more.

I want to hear how I'm the most wonderful thing in the

world. I want to hear that I'm important beyond time and death.

I want to shout out, 'MORE. MORE. *MORE*.'

But if I say anything it'll spoil it.

It's like that feeling when you know that if you take one mouthful you'll never stop eating.

And that's dangerous. You could swallow the universe.

'You're stupid,' I say.

'You're goddamn right I am,' he says. 'For a minute I thought I was falling in love with you, but now that you've pointed it out, love is stupid as well as pathetic.'

I bite my lip. 'Yeah. Pathetic and stupid and puerile.'

Fletcher starts to giggle. An uncontrollable, manic kind of snorting. He yanks a piece of honeysuckle from the climber that straggles over the wall.

I start giggling as well. Yes, it's pathetic and stupid and puerile and laughable. And I'm giggling and laughing and swallowing my laughter and choking and tears are running down my cheeks because it's so stupid and nothing about anything is funny. And I've promised myself I will always laugh with Fletcher. But it's so not funny that it's funny.

'Don't shower me with spit again, Dani,' warns Fletcher.

'Definitely no more pathetic, stupid spit,' I say.

Fletcher goes down on one knee, holds up a spray of honeysuckle and says in a husky voice, as if he's a hero in a romantic film, 'Please accept this stupid rose as a laughable token of my undying patheticness and stupidity.'

I laugh and choke and flap my hands.

Fletcher shoves the sprig of honeysuckle up towards my face.

Under my nose.

I breathe it in.

And nothing is funny any more.

My breath catches.

I swallow.

I blink.

The smell of honeysuckle.

Suddenly I'm back in the room.

The smell of honeysuckle is wafting in through the open window.

The Alien wails from the galaxy of MACS0647-JD.

The room of honeysuckle and death.

I can hear planks being unloaded, truck engines revving, iron gates screaming, and the smell is choking me. I'm leaning out of the window. The wall is covered in honeysuckle. I read the sign on the wall opposite, stencilled in old painted letters, Berkshire-based Wood Products, *and the smell of honeysuckle and the smell of death.*

My hand flies to my throat.

Fletcher grips on my arm. '*Dani!*' he yells.

I swallow.

I try to speak. *But I'm in the room.* I throw my arm out to see if I can stop myself. The smell is too strong. All I can do is try to push the sprig of honeysuckle away from my face.

'Oh, God,' says Fletcher, 'you're back there.'

His voice is coming from far away.

'Use it, Dani. Don't fight it,' Fletcher begs. 'Tell me where you are. Look around.'

I'm in the room. It smells of death. There are flies everywhere. The door is locked. I can't get out. There's a yard opposite. There are letters stencilled on the wall. I trace them on the grimy glass of the window.

'Berkshire-based Wood Products,' I croak out.

They're loading wood. I'm in the room. I can't get out. There's a body lying across the door.

And there's something else at the corner of my memory, something that I want to say, but it's too horrific to understand. I know who the body is. I know it, and I cannot know it.

I won't know it.

'Is it the name on a paint can? Varnish?' Fletcher is on his feet. He lets go of my arm. 'Berkshire-based Wood Products. Is it a shop, Dani?'

He's got his phone out. He's typing things into it. His face is pointed like an arrow flying at the sun.

I want to call to him from inside the room. I want to feel his pathetic, stupid love and his puerile arms around me.

'Whose body is it?' he says. 'Man? Woman? What're they wearing? How did they die? Tell me more about the varnish.'

He's not looking at me, just typing and searching on his phone.

I know who the body is.

'Is it a place?'

I know it, and I cannot know it.

'I'll find out where it is!'

I refuse to understand.

Oh, Fletcher.

'OK, come out of the room, Dani,' says Fletcher. 'We've got a clue. We can do this. Everything is going to be OK now.'

He sits down beside me on the broken bench, then jumps up again, suddenly excited. 'I think I've found out where you were.'

He holds his phone out to me. It's a blur. I can't even lift my arm to take it.

He sees.

He puts his arms around me.

'It's OK, babe,' he says. 'I've got you. You can come out now. I'm here. I won't ever leave you.'

I blink. The walls of the room start to fade. I'm looking at Fletcher's smartphone.

He's pointing at a photo of a block of 1930s flats and a website that says:

Berkshire Council Flats
Sold Off to Private Company

The old-fashioned brick flats will receive a government grant as part of a new deal with an American holding company. A spokesperson for the group said, 'We can regenerate the area, modernize the flats, repoint brickwork and revarnish all the lovely old woodwork. Our aim is to bring life back into this once-thriving community.'

I shake my head.

'No?' he says.

The flats look as unfamiliar as Mercury.

Fletcher's shoulders slump.

I take a tiny sip of breath.

I know who the body is.

'Never mind, we'll find out.'

I shut my memory against it.

The honeysuckle. The smell of death.

I refuse to remember.

'I'll find out everything, I promise you,' says Fletcher.

He puts his arm around me.

I sit on the broken bench and lay my head on his shoulder.

'I'll save you, if it's the last thing I do.'

23

Fletcher means it.

He texts me during Reflection Hour. *You said something about noises in the room. Tell.*

I text back: *Planks being unloaded, truck engines revving, iron gates screaming.*

During Occupational Therapy he texts again. *Planks being unloaded could be a building site.*

I text him: *Could be but I don't think so.*

Another text during supper. *Been thinking, why not a building site? Engines fit in with that, and so does the Wood Products sign.*

I reply, *Cos I didn't hear anything else, only planks.*

True, he texts. *Building sites have diggers and cranes and gravel and workers.*

After Think First, I get: *OK. Going with wood only. What about a sawmill?*

Maybe, I send back.

☺ ☹ ☹

By Lights Out, he's sent: *I'm so excited. I think it's got to be either a sawmill, a DIY place, a company that builds pallets or similar, a garden centre or a woodyard. All those fit in with planks, lorries and gates.*

⊘ 🖐 💣

I wake up to more.

Lee has flogged all the laptops. Meet in the library tomorrow?

I roll over and try to get back to sleep. My stomach hurts. All of me hurts.

The Mystery Of The Body. In the library after CT?

I pull the duvet over my head.

Say yes.

My phone pings.

I love doing all this. Come up to the library. I'll help you up the stairs.

Reluctantly I text back. *OK.*

Immediately he replies. *I think I AM falling in love. Pathetic, puerile, stupid and laughable maybe, but still love. Your very own Sherlock.*

🌑 ☠ 🖐

In the morning, halfway through Circle Time, during fag/ coffee break, in the slanty, vast, long library, Fletcher puts me down. He's breathing hard. His hair flops over his face. His T-shirt sticks to him. I can see the muscles of his chest outlined beneath the cloth.

'I'm heavy, aren't I?' I say.

He laughs. 'You wish.'

'You're sweating,' I point out.

'It was the stairs, not you.'

Always gallant. So gallant.

'Let's get started. We've only got about twenty minutes.'

We settle down on a bench. The same bench as before. It seems to welcome us. The computer flicks on at just a touch. Everything seems waiting, ready to share deep, dark secrets.

'I've got a really good feeling about today,' says Fletcher.

And before I can answer, he puts his arms around me. He pulls me into his sweaty chest. He's warm. His heart is thumping. He smells of boy and sweat and roll-ups.

'I've never done that before,' he says. 'I've comforted you and carried you. I've never just hugged you, just to hug.'

'Am I too thin?' I ask.

'You are you,' he says, and buries his face in my hair.

But I hate being me.

'Am I too fat?' I say.

Fletcher lets go of me. 'Let's start,' he says.

I wish we could just sit here and hug. I like the smell of sweat and smoke. Maybe I didn't say what he wanted to hear.

'I went for woodyards and DIY centres. They seemed more likely. Sawmills probably only exist where they build log cabins.'

Maybe I should have hugged him back.

'I looked for ones that featured in news headlines about finding small children,' he adds very softly.

Google throws up a list of websites.

'Looked?' I say.

'I've been searching on my phone all night. I've hardly slept. There's one I want you to see.'

I put my arm through Fletcher's.

'Even if I'm too fat or too thin, it was nice being hugged,' I say.

Fletcher looks at me. Honey swirls in his eyes; his face is firelight. 'Really?'

'Really.'

He shuffles closer to me on the bench.

'We can share the screen,' I say.

Fletcher puts an arm around me.

'And I don't care if you do have head lice.'

Fletcher gently squeezes my Thinness.

It feels good. And my Alien is snoring. Its eighty thousand eyelids gently twitch. Deep dreams of moonbeams and stardust.

Fletcher clicks the mouse.

Google throws up 230,972,035 search results for 'News. Child. Wood. Timber. Lewisham. Body'.

'Here it is.' Fletcher scrolls down and taps on a link.

It's a web page of a news item, dated years previously.

And a picture.

It's a woodyard.

Across the high back wall of the yard, *BERKSHIRE-BASED WOOD PRODUCTS* is stencilled in peeling blue paint over whitewashed brick.

And the headline reads:

Timber Yard Horror

FOUR-YEAR-OLD FOUND IN ROOM WITH CORPSE. In a horrifying turn of events, workers find a four-year-old girl locked in a room with the body of her mother.

The body of her mother.

My mother.

I knew.

I knew.

I refuse to know.

The body of my mother.

Please, not my mother.

24

What's the point of a strategy? What's the point if there's no happiness out there in the world?

It's a big joke, all that going without food. All that careful counting, that calculation, that being on time and leaving last, and sussing out where the bathroom was in case I really couldn't make it through one meal without eating. And all the time there was no happiness to save up for. That's very funny. My Alien is laughing. He likes that kind of joke.

There is no point in points.

'I told you so,' he says. 'Outer Space is cold and empty. Now you know. The only good things out there are kind Aliens like me who are ready to be your friends.'

There's no point in anything.

FLIGHT TWO

COURAGE TO CHANGE

STEP FIVE
THE EXACT NATURE OF OUR WRONGS

25

At supper, Fletcher comes to sit with me.

He has no new ideas about how to console me. So he says, predictably, 'You need to talk about it, Dani.'

I agree with Einstein. The kind of thinking that gets you into a problem won't get you out of it. Fletcher has no new thinking to offer. He only has one big pathetic heart, his addiction and his codependent personality.

'We need to talk about what this means for you,' he says. 'So I think we should carry on sharing our experiences – maybe more of our worst ones – and see if we can work on this.'

See what I mean.

'What do you think?' he says.

I don't answer.

That newspaper article is my worst one.

The child – found dehydrated, emaciated and unable to speak – is believed to have been purposely subjected to imprisonment.

'I know it's taken some time and it's been tough,' says Fletcher, 'but we're getting somewhere. And if Judith is right, this may be a blessing in disguise. It may unlock the thing that stops you eating. Look, we found out who the dead body was.' He's choosing his words so carefully.

'My mother.'

He immediately realizes his mistake.

A blessing in disguise. Seriously?

'I mean, we found out something important,' he corrects himself.

He does not add: 'We found out that she deliberately locked you in a room and tried to kill you, which means she was a murderer and you were her victim. And she was much more cruel to you than my mother was to me. In fact, she was the cruellest kind of mother anybody could have, seeing as she tried to kill you. So not only were you alone and unlovable, but you were also disposable. In fact, she hated you so much that in trying to kill herself she decided to take you along too. Just for nothing. Because you were worth nothing. And whatever warped thinking was going on in her mind is not an excuse – even if she was mentally ill. Doing that can never be construed as love.'

As unequivocally pointed out by the news article:

It appears that the mother, thirty-seven-year-old
Caroline Carlton, locked herself and her child into the
room in what was a calculated, suicidal act of cruelty.

Instead, he says, 'And now we should be able to find out where the room was and what happened after that.'

Big deal.

'And then we have to find a way for you to get over it,' Fletcher says. 'I mean, that's the theory.' He's still trying so hard. 'You find out what has traumatized you, you accept it, then you heal.'

'So all I have to do is accept it?' I ask.

'Hey, well done,' he says. 'You actually spoke.'

Accept that I was unloved, that I was locked in a room, that I was helpless and small, and *my mum* did it.

And then get over it?

I can feel a tentacle sneaking around my shoulders.

'But you met me there,' says the Alien.

I turn my head slightly. I'm surprised to see that he's wearing dark glasses. I've never seen my Alien in dark glasses before.

'OK, so shall we try to accept that our mothers didn't love us?' says Fletcher.

His earnestness is so painful.

'I'll go first,' he says. 'I'll journal all the horrible things my mum did to me and then it's your turn.'

26

Lee is running a new scam. He's trying his hand at counterfeit money. It goes like this: you give him £100 real money and he'll get you £500 fake money. If you're a bit wary of this deal, he can reduce the amount. You give him £20 real money and he'll get you £100 fake cashback. As long as you do £400 'change up' for him.

'We all need to get ready,' Lee says. 'When we leave this place, we'll need to pay rent and be upright citizens and shop at Sainsbury's, and you can't do that on jobseeker's allowance.'

It's a convincing argument.

'So this is what you do,' Lee says. 'You take the twenty-pound notes I give you into the corner shop and you buy chewing gum. Then you get nineteen pounds plus some change back, which is real money, and you give me the gum and the change. Next time, you change the next twenty-pound note at another corner shop. You get the idea.'

This is what he means by 'change up'.

'This really works because the counterfeit money is sick,' he says, showing us a sample £20 note.

It's very realistic.

'The only thing you have to clock,' says Lee, 'is if they try to mark it with that black pen, because the fake money is on fake paper. But they've done a good job with the watermark and there's the silver thread going right through the notes.'

'My best advice is try to change it with old people,' he continues. 'They don't see too good, and are always in a hurry to go and have a cup of tea. Like, they can't be bovvered and they're bigger suckers.'

Right.

'The worst kind of person to change it with is a tough-looking checkout bitch – she'll check everything. That's all you need to know.' Lee clears his throat. 'You really need to take advantage of this deal while they're still printing fake money. Soon they'll move operations to other areas – or the banks will start to notice. This is your one and only chance to make a quick bit of clean cash.'

I don't know how many people at the centre will give it a go. Iggy says he's going for it and he'll try to pay for his treatment with it. He says that would be another kind of big joke, because as far as he's concerned the recovery programme we're getting here is as fake as the notes.

I don't know what to think. I don't know whether to go for the fake money or not.

When I ask Fletcher if he will, he says, 'You're goddamn right I will.'

27

The saddest thing about addiction is when you compare reality to the way things could have been. I'm sure this has some kind of psychological name. Judith probably knows it.

It's very painful when you think of all the things you could have done. All the chances that have been swallowed into the pit. We were all born so beautiful, so loving. It's even more painful when other people point this out. Repeatedly.

Kerstin always makes sure she does.

During her visits we sit in the conservatory in the visitors' centre.

The sun shines in through the glass. Kerstin is very hot and takes off her cardigan. I'm always cold. Even sun shining through conservatory windows has no effect on me.

'So how's it going?' asks Kerstin.

'OK,' I say.

'I'm so glad you got a place here,' she says.

I don't know why *she* should be glad. But I don't say anything.

'So how's it going?' Kerstin asks again.

'OK.' I can't distract myself with dreams of endless piles of fake money any longer.

'How's the food? Is it any good here?'

Weird question.

Maybe I could ask her about checking out the story in the newspaper. That faint ray of hope I've been nurturing breaks free.

Maybe it wasn't me.

'You're looking great,' she says.

Maybe that four-year-old was somebody else.

I know I'm not looking great. But I smile at her. It was kind of her to come and see me.

And the body was not my mother.

'So I need to tell you all about this new boyfriend I have,' says Kerstin.

It could be true.

The Alien pops up from behind her chair, pulls a stupid face and sticks his tongue out at her.

'He's really buff and fit and lush.' Kerstin adjusts her skirt in a sexy way. 'And I fancy the pants off him.'

The Alien smiles a sly grin.

I mean, it really could be true.

'But there are a few things about him that worry me.'

She doesn't wait for me to ask what.

'You see, the thing is, he's kind of arrogant, and that makes him very attractive and fanciable and all that, but sometimes he doesn't really listen to me.'

I'm going to believe it wasn't me. Just for now.

The Alien moves out from behind Kerstin's chair into the middle of the conservatory. It makes very lewd, hip-thrusting gestures at her with some of its rude Alien parts.

I start to cheer up.

'When you're better,' says Kerstin, 'we can work on getting you a boyfriend too. I'm using this great dating site. There are loads of guys on it who all want to hook up for a bit of fun. They won't mind if you've been in here.' She gives me an I Am So Free Of Prejudice smile. 'We don't have to tell them you're mental anyway.'

'Thanks,' I say.

'It's so much fun. I can help you write your profile. And you're so thin! All the guys are going to fancy you like crazy.'

There are some biscuits (exactly four) on the table.

'Have a biscuit,' I say. Perhaps I can score a point while she's talking about dating and how mental I am.

'So, babes,' says Kerstin, 'this is what we're going to do. In order to get you back into having lots of fun, which is exactly what you need, I read up all about anorexia. I even watched stuff on YouTube – see what a good friend I am! So the thing is, it's all about self-hate – that's why you do it.'

I look at her. I'm trying really hard not to look at the Alien. If I look at him, he'll make me giggle. Also, she's about to pick up a biscuit.

'So what you have to do is stop the slimming,' says Kerstin. 'It's very simple.'

I decide to humour her. 'OK,' I say. 'So how do I do that?'

'Right,' says Kerstin in full-on helpful mode. 'We're going to write down a list of all the things that are great about you, OK?'

'OK,' I say.

'Fantastic,' says Kerstin. She puts her hand out, grabs a biscuit and stuffs it into her mouth.

OH, YAY!

Then she gets out a pen and pad and says, 'I knew you wouldn't think of this, so I've come prepared!'

I watch her chewing and swallowing. It was a Viennese sandwich. They contain eighty-two calories per biscuit.

'Let's do it then,' says Kerstin. 'I'll write it down – that'll make it easier for you. So, I think you're pretty.'

She writes on the list: *Pretty*.

'Now it's your turn,' says Kerstin.

'And I'm thin,' I say facetiously.

'Totally,' she says. 'Being thin is great – boys totally love skinny girls.'

She writes: *Thin*.

The Alien mouths out, 'Are all your friends stupid?'

'And you have a nice personality,' continues Kerstin.

I flick him a look which says: What friends?

Kerstin writes: *Nice person*.

'Your turn,' she says.

'I have good friends like you,' I say. This makes the Alien fall over and roll on the floor in spasms of laughter.

She writes: *Nice friends*.

'Now, what are you good at?' says Kerstin.

I think about that. 'I'm good at spotting all kinds of fake things,' I say.

She writes down: *Not cheap. Likes quality stuff.*

'What about sports or painting?' Kerstin asks.

'I'm not much good at painting,' I say. 'But I'm quite good at sports – at least, I don't give up.'

'Great,' she says. 'Sports is really good.'

On The List Of Great Things About Dani, she writes down: *Ready to have a go.*

'And you have lots to give other people,' says Kerstin.

She quickly adds:

Quite interesting.
Can be funny at times.
Not moody.
Not usually boring or self-centred.

Then she strikes the final line through.

'How are we doing?' I ask.

Kerstin reads out the list. As she reads it, she picks up another biscuit and bites half of it off. The second biscuit is a slice of caramel shortbread. They're 205 calories each. She's consumed 287 calories in the space of five minutes.

One rule of my strategy is I can never get more than one point at a sitting – which is a pity, because if Kerstin stuck around long enough, I might make enough points to have a chance of being happy today. Plus I'd have a list of great things about me made at the same time.

'Right, you're going to Blu-Tack this list to your mirror,' says Kerstin. 'Then every time you look in the mirror and think you're fat or ugly, you read through the list of great things about yourself. Then you can try some aphorisms too. What aphorisms shall we make up for you?'

'What's an aphorism?' I say, like I don't know.

If I humour her and pretend to be an idiot, she might eat another biscuit. Luckily I've remembered that if I can get someone to eat a biscuit or something else that contains over 100 calories – that they might not otherwise have eaten – I earn an extra point. I didn't just make that up.

So, rather daringly, I pick up the plate and push it a little closer towards her. There's another caramel slice on it. The Alien jumps out from behind a retro sideboard and looks on in a really melodramatic, shock-horror, fake way. He clasps a tentacle over his mouth and makes saucer eyes.

'OK,' says Kerstin, 'we'll do one aphorism this visit. Then next time I come I'll give you another one. I think you should say, "I am beautiful." OK?'

'OK,' I say.

'So after you've read the list which is Blu-Tacked on your mirror, you say, "I am beautiful" ten times. OK?'

'OK,' I say.

'I really don't know why you haven't tried doing this before.'

Neither do I.

'It's going to be so awesome when you start getting better.'

'I am getting better,' I say. 'I had six of those biscuits this morning.'

Sometimes if you say stuff like that, it encourages others to eat as well.

I wait hopefully.

Kerstin picks up another biscuit.

See.

The Alien does a Highland fling of victory.

'Oh well,' she says. 'Then I guess I shouldn't worry about having another.'

She puts the caramel slice in her mouth and crunches. I'm so happy. I get another point. All I have to do is keep her talking for ten minutes to make sure she doesn't go out and vomit. Shouldn't be too hard. I'm doing quite well today.

'I think I should eat something healthier than biscuits though, Kerstin,' I say. 'Is there an aphorism to help me do that?'

'Right,' she says. 'I'm going to think of one.'

'Yes, please do,' I say.

A new thought has just struck Kerstin whilst chewing the biscuit. 'You could eat lots of fruit. Fruit has no calories. You won't mind that, will you?'

'That's true,' I say. 'Fruit has fewer calories.'

'Next time I visit I'm going to bring a whole bunch of grapes and – what's your favourite fruit? Do you like apples? They're really good for you.' She doesn't wait for my reply. She seems to be mentally ticking things off on a list of what she's going to do for me.

I wait politely and don't remind her that addiction clinics have canteens.

She jumps up and gives me a hug. 'It's been so great to see you, Dani,' she says. 'And it's so great to know you're doing so well. Don't forget all the tips I've given you! I'll call you with the best aphorisms to promote eating when I've done some more research. And I'll tell you all about all the buff boys I'm dating.'

I glance at the clock. Just keep her talking.

Should I ask her about the newspaper article now? Even though it might spoil everything?

'I'd like the eating aphorism now so I can get well quicker and start dating sooner,' I say.

'OK,' she says. She pulls a face and reflects.

That was definitely the right thing to say.

She sits down again and gets out her pen and paper.

'You can say, "I love food" ten times before every meal, and do tapping. I'll write it all down. You tap your forehead when you say: I love food. Like this.' She demonstrates tapping for me, then starts scribbling a full set of instructions.

Only one minute left.

The Alien is going crazy.

'FABULOUS!' I scream.

Kerstin is beaming. 'Great,' she says. 'You know I'd do anything for you, Dani, just anything. All you have to do is ask.'

'There is one thing,' I mumble.

Dare I? Surely now is the right time?

'Anything,' she says.

'Could you check out a news article for me?' My heart starts pounding. 'It's kind of urgent and important.' I rush the rest of the request out before I lose courage. 'We all have to do a life timeline in here and I need more information. It's not just that. I was put in care, you see, and I've had a really scary memory out of nowhere. From a very early time I don't remember. It would really help me. You might need to ring someone up to make enquiries.'

'Just email me the details, darling. I'm committed to making sure your recovery is a total success!'

'Thanks,' I say, a bit overwhelmed. How easy was that?

If only the article was about an entirely different four-year-old.

'This visit has been a *huge* hit, don't you think? I'm such an awesome friend to you!' she says, swinging her massive designer bag over her shoulder.

She blows me an ostentatious air-kiss.

On the way out, she picks the last biscuit off the plate.

'Yes,' I say. 'It really has been a hit – it's been totally terrific. Please do come again.'

28

There are no free meal tickets. One way or the other you pay for everything.

After Kerstin leaves, I have to face the fact that I was really mean and fake and possibly murderous to her. It doesn't make it any better that she was unaware of how cruel and mean I was.

I know, and the Alien knows, and you can't hide from yourself.

So I take another kind of inventory after she's gone. On the piece of paper she left, I draw another column and I write:

- You're sneaky.
- You're mean.
- You laugh at other people and pretend to agree with them.
- You always think they're patronizing you.
- You make them eat when they may not want to.
- You encourage them to get fat.
- Biscuits are full of hydrogenated fats and empty calories, and you've contributed to their heart disease.

- *You're killing them.*
- *You're hateful.*
- *You don't deserve any of the points you got this morning.*
- *If you don't text Kerstin and tell her she doesn't have to bother coming again, you can't keep the points.*
- *You must apologize to her.*
- *She was so kind and really wanted to help you.*
- *And she agreed so willingly to look into that news article.*

I text her and say: *Hi Kerstin. I don't deserve to be your friend. You were really genuine today, and I don't deserve that kind of treatment. Please don't worry about me. You don't need to come again.*

I stop and then I add: *If you don't want to. I will miss you.*

Then I add: *I'm going to send you a link for the information I need. Thank you so much for agreeing to research it for me. You really are an awesome friend.*

I delete *I'll miss you.*

I'm not sure that I'll miss her. But I also don't know that I won't miss her. I don't add it back though, because even if it turns out to be true, it seems a bit manipulative and this text has got to be totally genuine if I'm going to keep the points.

I press 'send'.

It sends.

And I start missing her.

29

I get a letter from Fletcher.

Dear Dani,

I'm doing the journaling as promised — all
that stuff about accepting our mothers didn't
love us. I've decided to get way more shit out
of my head about my own mother than you'll
probably want to hear. Sorry to dump it on
you. You don't have to read it all. Just writing
it down has shifted it for me. I think it'd be
good if you could do some journaling too. Here
goes.

1) She gave my things away without even
asking me. Though later she claimed she did
ask me. Maybe she threw them away. They
were always the things I really wanted to

keep too. If I was really upset and moaned about it, I got told they were never <u>really</u> mine to begin with, because I didn't earn any money, so they'd all been paid for by someone else.

2) She noticed every bodily function I had, and embarrassed me by mentioning them in company, like how often I did a shit or left the toilet seat up or missed out on showering. She always put it like she was really concerned, because maybe I had bowel cancer or something, so other people didn't guess she was being mean to me.

You can probably stop reading here. It's all a bit personal. Sorry about that.

3) I never had any privacy. She would regularly go through my things. She liked to dig into my feelings and ask nosy questions, like if I'd had sex yet.

4) She'd do things absolutely against my wishes, even when I'd told her not to do them.

5) She complained that nobody took any notice of her and that nobody loved her, even when I was the only person in the room. Then she would take pains to tell me that she'd been treated in a <u>very</u> loving way by some

random person. She would go on and on about it at every opportunity. Like how AMAZING it was that someone had been SO <u>KIND</u> to her and that they must <u>REALLY</u> LIKE her. She might even call these people her 'adopted sons' if they were my age - which they usually were. Whenever she did that there was this little teasing smile dancing somewhere across her lips.

6) She treated me as if I was useless, especially if there was an area where actually I wasn't. Like if she needed help downloading some software for her computer, she'd make comments like 'I really need to get an expert to do this' or 'It's no good - you'll only make it worse.' Or she'd greet my reassurances that I could do it for her with comments like 'hmmm' or 'How interesting.'

Thanks so much for sticking with this - if you've got this far.

7) If I confronted her about any of that, she'd use it as an excuse to start drinking. The next day when she'd sobered up, and after I'd given her some time to get rid of the hangover, and I'd ferried lots of tea and coffee up to her room, she'd tell me that I

really didn't like her at all and that that had upset her so much she'd had to try to make herself feel better by drinking – that it was all my fault, and now she was ill. Then she'd turn on me and say that I REALLY MUST STOP ACTING AS IF SHE HAS A DRINK PROBLEM. SHE DOES NOT HAVE A DRINK PROBLEM. If I persisted and said she was drinking too much and I was worried, she'd sulk and say, 'So I'm _ALWAYS_ drinking, am I?' or 'So you've _NEVER_ seen me sober, ever?' and 'So I'm a _TOTAL_ FAILURE as a mother, am I?'

That's all for now. I feel much better for writing it all down. Part of me still doubts that I really experienced all this. That's why doing this helps. Today I'm trying to get it clear.

Oh, and last but not least:

8) If I crawled away into a corner just to be alone and maybe play games on my phone, she'd find me out and assault me with her well-meaningfulness. Like, she'd say, 'Surely you're cold here – you must move to the front room.' 'Are you trying to hide from me?' 'There's not enough light here. You won't be able to see anything. Move over

here. You'll spoil your eyesight.' 'That chair you're sitting on needs a cushion. Here's a cushion. Stand up – let me fix it for you. Actually, the chair's very old and delicate, and it belonged to my mother and is precious – perhaps it'd be best to sit on another chair. You know how destructive you are. I'll fetch you a different one from the front room, seeing as you don't want to sit in there with me.

Thank you.

Fletcher

PS

Once I got dumped by this girl. I was broken-hearted that she couldn't love me. But that wasn't the whole truth. I realize now that I was broken-hearted about reality. Her rejection confirmed everything my mum had told me: I was worthless and unlovable. I realized then that the world, which should be lovely and kind and trustworthy, was a lie. I wasn't heartbroken about the girl so much as heartbroken about the world.

PPS

Oh, and my mum was actually quite jealous. Any time I got anything nice, she would try to get it from me or get a better one for herself.

OK, that really is all.
Thanks again for staying with this, Dani.

X F

30

Fletcher finds me in the canteen, trying to score some points. He's in a different mood. He doesn't say, 'Let's share your worst thing. Let's share your best thing. Let's go to the library. Tell me a secret fear. Tell me a secret hope.'

He jumps in front of me. There's that line across his face. He's been running. Sweat trickles down his cheek.

'I was looking for you,' he pants.

I don't understand.

'Let's go for a walk,' he says. 'I need to talk.'

Going for a walk isn't easy when you feel as weak as I do.

'Let's go for a sit,' I say. I laugh.

The joke falls flat.

'No, a walk,' he says.

'OK,' I say.

'I'll walk,' he says, 'and you sit.'

He picks me up, and I sit in his arms. He walks down the back steps out into the garden and through the little gate at the side, on to the tennis lawns where Judith encourages us to play. Probably to underline her point about life and tennis.

He carries me all the way round the first tennis court to the little viewing pavilion. Then he sits me down on a bench. I unlace my arms from around his neck. I can feel the heat of his skin against the inside of my arms. I can smell him. He still smells of roll-ups but somehow more male and more fresh.

For a brief instant, I think I could love someone who smells like that.

He stands in front of me breathing hard. I weigh less than when he carried me up to the fifth floor, but I guess carrying me down two flights of stairs and around a tennis court isn't that easy either. His T-shirt is creased and wrinkled. The muscles of his cheek tighten. He seems to be curiously smooth-skinned.

'I have to tell you,' he says, panting, 'that we can still make it.'

He drops down on one knee beside me and wraps his arms around my chest. He buries his face in the side of my neck. I'm full of some kind of new energy. I find that I'm putting my arms around him quite naturally.

'I missed you this morning,' he says.

'I didn't come down to breakfast,' I say.

He's going to say something about eating. I know it. It's so boring. When really it's about points.

'I don't care,' he says. 'I just missed you.'

Somehow we're at a place we've never been to before.

The sun is high above us. Just like we're an ordinary boy

and an ordinary girl falling in love by an ordinary tennis court.

It's so strange to feel ordinary.

I never thought I'd like it.

We could even be happy. It might be possible. Without points. Judith could be wrong. Life, after all, might just be a game of tennis.

Suddenly I'm glad I came to Daisy Bank Rehab. I'm glad I've had to deal with all its fakery and synthetic, pretentious rubbish. I'm even glad about Carmen. Because I've met Fletcher.

And, right now, he feels like the most real thing in the world.

'Do you remember what we promised?' he whispers into my neck.

Suddenly I'd quite like to talk. Talking could be fun. I could tell him that I remember everything about our promise. And especially how naked it felt to be real.

Fletcher seems to pick up on that. He's kneeling on the floor of the pavilion with his face buried in my collarbone. He quickly gets up and sits down beside me.

'Do you remember, Dani?' he asks.

'Yes,' I say.

'I need you now, Dani,' he says, 'and you're not getting any better. You're not getting stronger and I need you so badly.'

I don't want to spoil this new mood. A crazy energy spirals around us. I like it. But I don't understand.

'It's just that I never saved my mum,' he says.

'How could you have?' I ask.

'I thought if I tried hard enough. If I ignored all the cruel comments. If I mopped up after her. If I threw out all the empty bottles. If I cleared up the mess. If I loved her long enough and hard enough. If I poured myself into her. If I stayed her little boy and hid all the signs of growing up from her. If I accepted the reality she wanted. If I stopped being me and devoted all my energy, my caring, my thinking, my time, my soul. If I did all that I thought I could save her.'

I think about that.

In a weird way, it sounds like trying to control things, not accepting what was going on.

'You mean, you thought you could stop reality from happening?' I ask.

He nods his head, then smiles. 'Yeah, I know, like I was God.'

I smile too at the thought of one teenager going to war with reality.

'She died anyway,' he said. 'Drank herself to death. To me, that was proof of how useless I was. How love is just not enough.'

'Why are you telling me this?' I say.

'I just need you. I need you to be there for me. I need you to remember what we promised,' says Fletcher.

'I remember,' I say.

'And it's like it's happening all over again,' says Fletcher.

I look at him. I don't understand.

'I've been trying so hard,' says Fletcher. 'I've been fighting reality all this time, but you've got that same look about you that my mum had before she died. And I don't think I'm enough any more. And love isn't enough. And I can't stop you from dying.' His shoulders slump.

The quality of the sunlight fades; it turns from sunflower yellow to acid lemon.

Leaves stir in the trees around the tennis court. I don't look at them. I know the Alien is hiding behind one of their trunks. I'm tired of the Alien. I want a real friend. A friend like Fletcher. But it all feels far too painful suddenly. Too difficult.

'Let's go back,' I say.

'Back to our deal?' A spark lights up in his eye.

I meant back to the centre.

31

I force myself to write to Kerstin. I'm only doing it to please Fletcher. Probably. If I show that I'm working on finding out why I'm so ill then he can stop worrying. Possibly. It will mean that I'm not going to die. Or at least I'm trying as hard as he is to keep myself alive.

I write the email.

Dear Kerstin,

How are you? How's the newest boyfriend(s)? I hope he's/they're treating you well.

Thank you so much for always visiting me. And thank you very, very much for offering to do a bit of investigating for me. It really is very, very important. I'm trying to find out who I am and what happened to me in an effort to heal. I'm stuck in a horrible nightmare. I don't know what to think. And I can't seem to eat or sleep or move on. I found this article in the *Lewisham Local*, but I don't have any idea of the date or place this happened:

Timber Yard Horror

FOUR-YEAR-OLD FOUND IN ROOM WITH CORPSE.
In a horrifying turn of events, workers find a four-year-old girl locked in a room with the body of her mother . . .

You can read the whole article if you Google that first line.

I'm hoping this poor little girl wasn't me. It's freaking me out a bit (a lot) because I've remembered snatches of things about being locked up in a room.

Thing is, they changed my name, so I have no way of knowing. I literally have no memory of my early years. I've tried searching online for more details, like who and what and where and when, and mostly why, but we're not really allowed laptops and mobiles in here and I'm finding it difficult and exhausting. It's almost impossible to make private phone calls during office hours. Really I need someone to try and find out more/anything. Maybe Lewisham Social Services might be ready to tell you something? I was put in care with them and renamed Dani.

If I could just find out my real name that would be a start. I think my first name was Isla (Izzy), but I'm not sure if I've just imagined that. It has only just occurred to me as I am writing this! Oh, God, I'm so confused.

I'm sure the British Library would have records of any other news articles. The courts might have records too – name changes, custody orders, etc. There must be some record of my mother's birth certificate somewhere. Could you try and find out? The woman in the article (my mother?) was called Caroline Carlton and was thirty-seven.

I really need this info urgently and it would seriously help my recovery. Without it I can't move on. I wouldn't ask, but I know you care and have offered to help.

Thank you so much. I'm really so grateful.

Best Love,

XXX Dani

32

It's Circle Time. Fletcher isn't here.

That's bad. If you're a state-funded client and you miss Circle Time, that's very bad.

It means you're not committed to your recovery.

Tony says: 'Many meetings, many chances; few meetings, few chances; no meetings, no chances.' And he means it.

Even Lee doesn't miss Circle Time. Though he rocks up totally stoned.

I think about that. Maybe it means at some level even Lee wants to get better. I don't know why I'm so shocked. Doesn't everybody want to get better ultimately?

For the first time I really look at Lee. He might have been good-looking, if his face wasn't pitted all over and discoloured.

I smile at him.

He smiles back.

I raise an eyebrow.

He knows what I mean: Where's Fletcher?

Lee raises one shoulder and drops it: Don't know. Don't ask. Don't care.

Circle Time drags. I want it to fast-forward and finish so that I can go and look for Fletcher.

When I find him I'm going to shake him. I'm going to tell him it's stupid to miss Circle Time. I'm going to shout in his face and ask him, 'WHAT THE HELL IS GOING ON?'

I'll order him to 'GET A GRIP AND FIX UP.'

I feel rage burning somewhere in my belly. It's hot and hurting. If Fletcher keeps missing Circle Time he'll get thrown out. Then what will he do? He has nobody. He has nothing. He's terrified of being alone. Where will he go? He's been living on the streets. He's stupid.

I must talk to him.

I must devote my energy, my caring, my thinking, my time to get him to really SEE.

'First, let's go around the circle and say how we're feeling today,' says Judith. 'I'll start. Hi, I'm Judith. I'm your psycho-dynamic counsellor and today I'm feeling hopeful.'

'Hi, Judith.'

The next person takes up the baton. 'Hi, my name is Jonny. I'm an addict. Today I'm feeling . . .' Pause. Longer pause. Nervous laugh. 'I'm just checking in with myself.' More nervous laughter. 'OK, today I'm feeling neurotic.'

'Hi, my name is Cormac. I'm an addict. Today I'm feeling freaky.'

'Hi, my name is Jennifer. I'm an addict. Today I'm feeling live-some.'

Cringe.

'Hi, my name is Shelley. I'm an addict. Today I'm not feeling too good.'

My turn.

'Hi, my name is Dani. I'm anorexic. I'm an addict. Today I'm feeling . . .'

What am I feeling? Worried, hopeless, panicky, angry, terrified, in shock, hopeless, dead, rotting, unmade, Alien?

I take a deep breath. 'Today I'm feeling happy.'

I must not lie. I must start to be real. I must stop being fraudulent. I force myself to lose one point.

Maybe I can change my answer? But the baton has moved on – my chance has gone. Today my real feelings must be denied: I will never be happy.

The baton satellites through confusion, hopelessness, anxiety and fear, until it gets back to Judith.

'Today, before we start our sharing,' says Judith, 'we'll have a Thunk.'

A Thunk, apparently, is a 'beguilingly simple question about everyday things' that cuts through the crap and helps you to look at 'reality' from a new perspective. It's Judith's strategy for introducing a 'cognitive input'.

Her Thunk for today is: 'Is there more Future or Past?'

A 'cognitive input' means a lecture from her on some psychodynamic theory. Judith likes being clever. She likes the sound of her own voice.

I don't.

She wants us to appreciate how very well qualified for this job she is.

I only want to find Fletcher and scream at him.

}}

I don't scream at Fletcher but I do find him.

After Circle Time I go to the library on the fifth level.

I'm hardly breathing. Exhausted. I climbed every step myself.

I knew he would be here, in the Coliseum of Cyberspace where he currently does his ongoing battle with reality.

Indulging his latest addiction: saving Dani.

The library is still slanted and vast. It still runs the length of the building. But today it's all beams and books and airy diagonals full of the smell of bloodshed.

I drop down at the computer hub beside him. I slump over, trying to catch my breath.

'Can we just stay quiet?' he says. 'No questions, just for a few minutes?'

Sunlight shafts through skylights. Ranks of brilliance.

'Why?'

'Because I'm feeling triumphant and I want the feeling to last.'

142

'About what?'

'I've transcended the here and the now. I've surrendered to my Higher Power and I've tasted paradise.'

'You missed Circle Time,' I point out.

'Can we please forget about that just for a moment? It was a sacrifice I had to make.'

'OK.' I nod. Forget everything. Forget the pain, the anger, the worry. Forget everything, why not?

Get high.

Step into a daring new world. Lit up with sunbeams. And get chucked out of the recovery programme.

Fletcher laughs, flicks open a computer.

'Why?' I say.

'No questions, remember.'

I need to wait until I can breathe a bit better anyway.

'I found out more,' he says.

I run my tongue over dry lips and wheeze out, 'Why didn't you come to Circle Time?'

'Shut up and read this.' Fletcher points at a web page.

'Fletcher?'

'Scroll down.'

Fletcher places his hand over mine and lifts it on to the mouse. A jolt of energy thumps into my chest. His hand is so alive, so warm.

With his finger on my finger, we scroll the wheel on the mouse until I don't know whose finger is whose. I feel his breath on my cheek. And the wheel turns. His finger on my finger. A shiver runs through me. It slices through the carpet.

I turn my head slightly.

He's so close.

I see continents of skin. Tiny hairs. The curve of his jawline. Some boyish stubble. I've never seen the universe of Fletcher before.

Fletcher turns towards me. An endless blue ocean fringed with eyelashes.

And the wheel turns.

A surprised smile.

Pulsing air.

'I love you, Dani. It's quite simple. I'd do anything for you. And I just love you.'

Hot breath. The light pools around us.

I lean in.

He leans in.

Our kiss is soft and volcanic and intense and thrilling.

And there's quite enough screen space for both of us.

And afterwards a blistering hurricane sweeps across the Sahara. A loop of electricity crackles from Fletcher to me to Fletcher again. And round and round.

I've never known any of this before.

Here we are. Alive. Just two teenagers kissing. In a library. During break.

Shivering and trembling and kissing.

Totally terrified.

And it's real.

It's really real.

34

Embrace the moment. Live for today. Lips and the smell of books. Sunshine in a slanty, angular library. Conquests in the Coliseum of Life.

And kisses. Sweet, sweet kisses.

Lee walks in and yells, 'Am I interrupting anything?'

Guiltily we spring apart.

'Shush,' says Fletcher.

'YO, SEX AND DRUGS AND ROCK 'N' ROLL,' shouts Lee.

'Go away,' I say.

The dust of the Sahara swirls.

'Please, Lee?' says Fletcher.

The wheel turns.

Relationships are forbidden. Clients at Daisy Bank Rehabilitation Centre must resign their place on the recovery programme if they form sexual relationships.

'I was just showing Dani what I found out,' Fletcher says, staring back at the computer screen.

Attendance at Circle Time is the one central commitment to recovery expected of all clients.

Lee grins.

'Look,' says Fletcher.

There on the screen it reads:

BERKSHIRE-BASED WOOD PRODUCTS ARCHES TIMBER LTD

London's Leading Timber Merchant

Timber, Sheet Material and Cladding Cut to Size

Call us on 020 3733 3801 or email your enquiry

Arches Timber Ltd

Phoenix Wharf

Mordly Hill Street

Lewisham

London SE4 9QQ

Opening Times:

Mon–Fri 7:00A.M.–5:00P.M.

Sat 8:30A.M.–5:00P.M.

'I did it, Dani!' Fletcher is exultant. 'I goddamn found out where that room was.'

STEP SIX
DEFECTS OF CHARACTER

35

I really should have screamed at Fletcher.

He must never miss Circle Time.

Never.

Never.

Never.

Never again. Certainly not on my account. Not on ANY account. HE MUST BE TOLD. I feel the panic rising inside me. Wobbling at the back of my throat. I can't swallow. I send him a text.

Listen. That was a dumb thing to do. I mean skipping CT. I know you're trying to help but NEVER NEVER NEVER do that again.

No reply.

Maybe now we've kissed he's going to avoid me. He doesn't even answer his phone.

The Alien starts laughing.

He's realized how ugly I am. He regrets kissing me. That is why kissing is not allowed. Kissing destroys things.

Screaming is so much better than kissing. I want to scream at Fletcher really loudly now.

But how can I go looking for him now we've kissed?

And start screaming?

It is so exhausting. I go to lie down.

Another letter has been pushed under my door. It's from him. He going to tell me he's made a horrendous mistake. He's going to insist we ask the centre to allocate us new partners. He's realized we can never be recovery buddies again.

I lie down on my bed, daring myself to open it.

One-way communication totally sucks.

You can't scream at a letter.

Even if you had the energy.

Dear Dani,

Today was so great in the library.

But why is it, when things go so well, I get jittery?

It's really bad. Almost panic. Really sweaty hands and heart jumping around everywhere. I can't sit down or stay still either. So I'm doing journaling again to see if it'll help. It did last time.

I'm sorry to dump it on you again. Especially because it was your turn to dump on me. I'm sorry too because I know I'm doing it in case you die. I'm being really selfish. But I have to be heard by at least one real person in this world that could, maybe (?), care about me. I'm so sorry it has to be you.

It's the lies, you see, that are worrying me now.

My mum lied. If she said she felt really deeply about something, you could bet your last piece of chewing gum she was lying. To outsiders she would lie deliberately, but always in a way that she could cover up. Once when she was being boastful, she told me, 'Lying is an art form. For example, if you are going to lie, be bold, go right up to some-one and look them square in the eye and lie your heart out.'

She'd boast: 'Only ever add one lie to a situation. Stir it in like you're blending cream into your coffee – you don't want it to curdle.' She'd laugh then at how clever she was. She'd say, 'Keep every other fact painfully truthful, and then seed your lie at the very heart of things.' She liked using 'the heart' as a meta-phor when she explained about lying.

But it wasn't <u>just</u> lying – like, fibs and that. She'd put dishonest interpretations on anything she wanted if it suited her. And she'd lie in advance to discount what I might say, before I even said it. It was impossible to catch her out. When I tried to tell my nan (before she died) how scared I was about Mum dying, Nan just said, 'Yes, your mum has told me you've invented "a thing" about her drinking.'

Mum would even lie to *me* after she'd been drinking. She'd say she'd had one teeny-weeny sip of gin and I'd gone ballistic. When I showed her the empty bottles, she sneered at me about the lengths I was prepared to go to, to demonize her, and swore blind I'd dug those bottles out of the rubbish.

When she really <u>couldn't</u> lie her way out of things, she'd say she'd 'only had a couple', but that was what happened when you had a 'child who was such a worry'.

I put the letter down. I pause. I consider. Is Fletcher telling me this because I am doing the same thing? Is this letter an accusation?

His mother was killing herself.

I am killing myself.

Fletcher tried to save her.

Fletcher is trying to save me.

An uncomfortable feeling, somehow like water going down a drain, starts at the back of my throat. Is Fletcher trying to explain why he is killing himself? Because of me? Or her?

I try to work it out.

The gurgling water empties into a lake.

Or is his letter a message of hope? See – our mothers hated us, but we have each other.

I long so much for that. I hate his mother. I hate my mother. But Fletcher is much nicer than I am. So I hate his mother more. His mother was hateful. Fletcher missed Circle Time. She could have loved him. Should have loved him. *She had all that time to love him.* Before he started killing himself. Suddenly the lake boils up, like a geyser of scalding water.

All the screaming spurts out.

I pick up a pen.

And she expected me to do everything she requested on command, and preferably at a time that was the most inconvenient for me. Like, just as I was leaving the house to go to school, she'd ask me to put out the rubbish, or look at the computer, which was 'playing up again, since <u>SOMEBODY</u> fiddled with it' and she needed it SO URGENTLY today – in fact, she was <u>REALLY ANNOYED</u>. It was <u>REALLY ANNOYING</u> – and a life or death matter – and she'd work herself up into a proper temper.

And I'd better fix it.

I drag the pen across the letter. I press hard. I grind the ball-point into the page in vicious lines. Up and back. Up and back. The paper rips.

The geyser spurts lethal jets of blistering water EVERYWHERE.

Of course there'd be nothing wrong with the computer, but she'd insist I run a full spyware check, and then I'd be late for school. I'd get detention and a telling-off. When I got back home afterwards, she'd tell me in THAT voice, 'The school rang again because you were late.' A voice that told me how embarrassed she was, what a disappointment I was. How, really, that was just EXACTLY what she expected of me.

Hateful.
Hateful.
Spiteful.
Vicious.
Up and back.

And she would invite herself along where she wasn't welcome. If I was going to go out and meet a friend she would insist on coming too. She was weirdly seductive to any lads I hung out with. It was really embarrassing. She would flutter her eyes and behave like a fifteen-year-old girl. I was scared to invite anyone home. So I stopped having friends. Then she would tell me that I was Jonny No Friends, that nobody liked me, and it was a miracle that she allowed me to hang around with her so much.

I put that page down, but before I pick up the next one, I scratch and scrawl all over it. Not just up and back. But round and down and round.

And round. Hard. Fast.

Craters open up.

I carve great holes.

Spots from the geyser land in drips on the writing. The ink smudges. I scrub the drips into his remaining words. The whole page is soggy, unreadable.

Falling apart.

She had all that time to love him.

I'm sorry, Dani. I'm just going on and on. Please forgive me.

Thing is, since I met you, you've given me hope. I am in such a dark place. I'm doing it to myself. It's really all so trivial. So what if my mother was horrible? Get over it. That's what everyone says. People are so mean. They're probably right. I don't know. But I can't seem to get over it. I can't seem to get a perspective.

I've fallen out of love with everything, with everyone.

I've reached a place where there are only lies. There is nothing to trust. And it's all my fault. When you believe everyone is untrustworthy, even yourself – especially yourself – you can't get over it.

But you are real, Dani.

Well, more real than anyone I've ever met.

And I think you could care about me if I fix up.

And I trust you.

X Fletch.

I read this last page again.

I run my thumb over the words 'more real than anyone'.

I run my thumb over my lips. They remember his kiss.

Then I text him. *Don't trust me. I've lied to you. I run strategies to make me feel better than other people all the time. My Alien laughs at everyone. He laughs at you.*

He texts back. *Only someone real could text me that.*

I text again. *I am mad at you. Mostly.*

He replies, *I probably deserve it.*

I reply, *OK. I will try to be worthy of your trust.*

Fletcher texts. *I feel such a mushroom.*

I text. *Mushroom?*

He replies, *Reared in the dark and fed shit. That was an attempt to use humour to get a sense of proportion. Ha ha. It's not even original. It's second-hand. I heard it somewhere. That's all I am: second-hand and not funny.*

You just accepted the reality your mum gave you.

Why do I obsess about her though?

Maybe you're still in the dark.

I am?

💣　☠　👎

Outer Space is dark. Maybe there is no waking up.

Maybe it's a choice, like in *The Matrix*. Here is the blue pill. Here is the red pill.

You choose.

36

Kerstin visits.

I'm hoping she may have news to tell me. Fletcher would like that.

'Hi, baby-head,' she says. 'How's tricks?'

It doesn't seem likely.

I sigh. I don't know why she bothers. I don't know why I bother.

'Anybody cute here? Anybody fanciable?'

'Everybody here is an addict,' I say. If she had news, she wouldn't start on that tack.

Kerstin laughs. She draws in her breath. 'Yeah, you're right – you should definitely aim higher.'

'I don't know,' I say.

'Nonsense,' she says all briskly. 'You just haven't met the right one yet.'

OK. There's no news. Kerstin wouldn't be able to wait this long before telling me what a great friend she's been.

If she had been a great friend.

But I need to make sure. 'Did you get my email?' I ask.

'Darling, I haven't been able to do anything about all *that* yet. I've been so busy. There's this new guy I've met, called Rod – he's totally dreamy.'

'Oh,' I say. 'That's nice. But will you be able to?'

'Yes, yes, of course, darling. I just need to think about it a bit. I hate doing things in a hurry.'

'Oh. OK. Thanks.' For some reason I'm surprised. Kerstin normally makes more of a show of being helpful. Especially after her last promises.

'Now back to you and that special person.' Kerstin shivers her shoulders as if *her* special person (presumably Rod) has draped a special-person arm around her and is blowing her special-person kisses. 'That's much more important.'

She leans forward and touches my hand. Perhaps she thinks that special-person-ness is catching.

I can already hear the Alien giggling and humming 'Some Day My Prince Will Come'.

OK. So no news on who I am, or why, or even if . . .

I try to refocus.

I vaguely wonder if everyone believes in THE ONE.

'There *is* hope, darling,' she says.

Bullshit. You're on your own. Fletcher was so right about that.

'Your knight in shining armour is out there waiting for you. You just need to believe it.'

No, he's not. Nobody is coming to save you. There are no heroes. There is no God. There is no meaning. Only you battling with yourself. All alone. And failing. And there is no final revelation that it all added up to anything. There is just this one messed-up life, and that's it.

And it's full of Kerstins.

'You *have* to believe!' says Kerstin.

What the hell does she mean? I don't even bother saying anything. She has got that smile playing over her top lip. That one Fletcher noted about his mum. It means she is getting one over on me. She has taken up residence on Planet Superior. She's believing in Beauty and Faith and Truth and Wisdom and Meaning and Love and Heroes and Happiness. Whereas I am not.

Anything I say now will sound morose and miserable and moronic. So I offer her a biscuit.

Luckily she accepts.

I hate myself.

I watch as she licks crumbs of a custard cream from the corners of her mouth, as she masticates and reassures herself that she is not the one with the problem.

I guess I should start composing my confessional text in advance. If I can be bothered. Even the thought of scoring a point has lost its appeal today.

I wish I was with Fletcher.

I push the plate at her and say, 'The Jammie Dodgers are really good.' Just out of spite. I don't even want the point. I can almost see her trying to think of a morally elevated spark of wisdom to throw at me.

'You should really read this book called *The Secret*,' she says. 'Basically, it tells you that the thoughts you send out return to you. You need to believe in a better future for yourself, Dani.'

Kerstin's tune has subtly changed from 'Some Day My Prince Will Come' into an upbeat remix of 'Every Little Thing Gonna Be All Right'.

'I'll bring you a copy next time I come.'

Oh God, so there's going to be a next time, is there?

'And look, I've written out a list of new aphorisms to keep you going!'

I start wondering how I can possibly discourage her from ever coming again.

'Just continue saying your aphorisms every morning,' Kerstin continues. 'You're really very pretty, you know.'

I don't know whether to say 'thank you' or throw my cup of coffee at her. Instead my eyes light on the biscuit plate.

Kerstin reaches out for another biscuit without me even suggesting it.

At some level, I start to cheer up. Today might be my lucky day after all.

'Yes,' continues Kerstin, 'once you've sorted out this chapter of your life, and have found the Right One, things will be a lot better.'

Wonderful. We are all now characters in *The Book of Life*. This chapter is entitled *Chapter Three: The Teenage Years, In Which Dani Becomes Anorexic and Goes to Rehab Then Cleans Up Her Act and Finds True Love.*

I don't think I want to recover if it means having to believe in all her Real-life Scripts.

There is no *Book of Life*.

There is no *Film of Me*.

This is it.

And I think I'm going to be sick.

And that's just it. That *is* the problem. If I do recover and I no longer have my Thinness, if I send my Alien off to live for ever in Outer Space without me, I will have to live in a world of Kerstins.

Multiple Kerstins, all promoting their own reality bubbles; all acting like reality isn't reality, spouting idealisms, playing out their perfect scripts, being better than everyone else, romanticizing their lives.

Real-life Scripts aren't real life. They're just ideas that make you feel good. That's all. Every addict knows about them. They allow you to be morally superior, even when you're shooting heroin. They're the ultimate form of denial. The Fletchers of this world have to learn to live without them, learn how to cope with being continually blasted by the Arctic breath of What Is. The Kerstins of this world have to have them to survive.

Hi, I'm Kerstin. I am sane.

I am healthy and it is you who has the problem.

I do not have weaknesses or addictions.

I believe in my Real-life Scripts.

Like:

- Everybody should always be loving and giving.
- We should be kind to everyone, even drug addicts.
- For every girl there is a Mr Right.

Addicts call Real-life Scripts like these Belief Systems.

BS for short.

They're just another kind of addiction.

From which no one is trying to recover.

37

I find Fletcher. We lie on the grass at the bottom of the garden, beside the compost heap. I'm trying not to go in with all guns blazing. I can't anyway. I'm too exhausted. My heart is doing that irregular shit thing it does so well. I'm trying hard not to panic. Judith says that panicking never helps anything. We need to take charge of our emotions. And for once, this is not all about me.

'Fletcher,' I say.

I find his hand in the grass beside mine. I hold it.

He does not reply. But he does squeeze my fingers, just a little bit.

I want to think about my Finger Thinness, about how my bones feel in the grasp of his hand. But I don't let myself.

'You can't give up,' I say.

Fletcher lets go of my hand.

There is a silence. I try to do mindfulness. I try just to listen to the spaces around the rustling of the leaves. Life is suffering. Detachment is the path. I fail.

'I emailed Kerstin again,' I say. 'I am trying.'

'Oh yeah.'

He's not fooled.

'You *can't* give up,' I say, hoping to get a better response.

'That's so totally goddamn awesome coming from somebody who gave up, like, aeons ago.' He sounds angry. No, not angry – just not here.

'Why are you so goddamn on holiday?' I try to lighten things up a bit.

'I've just stopped caring,' says Fletcher. He shifts, angles himself away from me. 'It's too painful.'

I reach out to grab his hand again.

'Don't give up on me, please?' I say. It comes out all wrong. Far too manipulative.

'Knock it off, Dani.' His words are acid dry. 'You're going to die. You know you are.'

Sandstorms whirl in some distant desert.

'I've done everything I can. I even found the woodyard. None of it was good enough,' Fletcher says. He almost laughs.

I sit up and look at him. Lips curled. Jaw clenched. Remote. I have to make him see HE CAN'T GIVE UP.

'Fletch?'

'All I want to do is use again. That's all there is.'

All there is? Great. What about me?

'Fletch?' This time I shake him. 'That's such crap. You sound like Lee.'

'Leave Lee out of this.' Fletcher throws my hand aside. 'At least he doesn't try to be what he's not.'

'So you're saying I'm trying to be what I'm not?' I ask.

'I'm not saying that.' Fletcher is defensive now. 'I'm just saying: can we leave Lee out of this?'

I sigh. 'I can leave anyone you goddamn like out of this. I just don't want you to give up.'

And I realize, suddenly, with terror, that I need Fletcher to carry on believing we can recover. I need to carry on believing that he can help me. I have become invested in his belief in me. If he gives up, I really *am* going to die.

So I say it. I try not to sound fake or guilt-trippy.

'If you give up, I am going to die.'

That is what I say. I'm not being melodramatic. I just know it's true.

'You're going to die anyway,' says Fletcher. 'That's just it. You decided that. You decided not to go back into the room. You decided because your mum was an arsehole you're going to throw your life away as well.' Fletcher picks up a bit of broken paving and hurls it at the honeysuckle.

'Well, look who's talking,' I say. I can't help it. It's a betrayal, I know.

'Thanks,' says Fletcher. He stands up and shakes my words off. 'In those letters, I was just trying to let you know that mothers aren't all goodness and light. That you need to challenge your own Belief System too.' He's smiling now, but I can see the rage behind his teeth. Hopeless, raw fury.

Touché.

'Sorry,' I mutter.

'If you start to recover, I'll go back to Circle Time,' says Fletcher in that jokey voice which I don't know how to take.

'I will try,' I lie. I don't know how to try.

Rage at Reality.

'OK. Try now,' says Fletcher.

He digs deep in his pocket and pulls out a pack of biscuits. It's one of those packs that are sealed in cellophane. The biscuits are broken and crumbled. They've obviously been in his pocket for a long time. Even if I was going to eat something, I don't think I'd choose bum-crumbled biscuits that have been in Fletcher's back pocket for ever.

Fletcher breaks the pack open. The crumbs fall on the grass. He tips pieces of broken biscuit into his open palm.

'Go on then.' He thrusts his hand at me. Aggressive.

I sit up. I try to salivate.

'You just want to save me so you can feel good enough,' I mumble. 'All your caring is just another form of selfishness.'

'Don't try to wriggle out of it,' he warns.

I have no saliva left. If I put those crumbs in my mouth, they'll stick to the roof of it like pieces of gravel. I hate biscuits. I love biscuits. I can't eat those biscuits. I ought to eat those biscuits. They might make Fletcher go back to Circle Time. I could eat a whole supermarket aisle full of biscuits. I ought to do that for him. Save us both. My throat feels like a trapdoor has flicked shut across the back of it. No crumb shall pass.

'Go on then,' he says. 'If you're so goddamn upset about me, eat the goddamn biscuit.'

I start to panic. I can feel a whirlwind opening up in my stomach. It's like a black hole. It's sucking everything into it. I can't put a biscuit in my mouth. My mother locked me in a room and threw away the key. My mother died and left me there alone. My mother never loved me. I can't put biscuits in my mouth. My mother wanted me to starve to death. With her rotting body. I want to save Fletcher. I want my mother to have loved me. Goodness and light. I must please my mother. I am going to die. I must die. She wanted it. I *have* to do what she wanted.

Then I will be loved.

I don't know what to do. I don't want to die.

'I'll help you, seeing as you've lost the power of movement.' Fletcher picks up half a biscuit. 'All you have to do is open your mouth, Dani. Can you do that for me?'

Sarcasm.

It hurts.

I can't open my mouth. I can't do that for him. I can't eat biscuits.

I panic.

Voices float across the garden from the centre. The noise of cutlery, crockery. It's lunchtime. If I eat the biscuits and somebody else has skipped lunch, I'll lose a point. I will not get my point. I WILL NOT GET MY POINT. Without points, I will never, never be lovable. I will never be good enough. Even Fletcher will abandon me.

'We need to talk about it,' I say.

'No, you need to eat it,' says Fletcher, 'and I need to go to Circle Time. We don't need to do any more talking – we've already tried to do Talking.'

But if we talk now, we could stop pretending that everything is OK; we could start talking about real things. I could find the right words.

Fletcher levers my mouth open. He places a piece of biscuit on my tongue.

'Now swallow,' he says.

I look at him. My hands are trembling. My chest is trembling. Tears well up in my eyes. I'm sweating. I can't do this. I can't swallow the biscuit. I'm fighting to let it stay there, half in, half out, balanced on my lower lip.

'You see,' says Fletcher. 'You see what I mean? You can't do it. Not even to save me. And that's why I've stopped believing. Why I've stopped caring. You want everyone to feel sorry for you *all* the time.'

I look at him. *What does he mean?* I never asked him to feel sorry for me.

'Yes, sorry for you,' he says. 'Sorry because you're so thin. Sorry because you were locked in a room with a dead body. Sorry because you're dying. Sorry because you found Carmen. Sorry because you had a lunatic mother. Sorry because you can't walk.'

Is that what he really thinks? Is that the truth? Am I doing all this so that somebody will feel sorry for me?

'So I'm gonna take all my sorriness back to the streets, and I'm going to get so goddamn shitfaced I won't feel sorry for nothing.' He laughs like a manic. Then he shudders.

And I realize he's right. I do want people to feel sorry for me. Everybody should feel so sorry for me. The world should stop turning and shed tears, all for me.

He is right.

I want violins. The whole lot.

But being pitied is so patronizing. I can take care of myself. I don't want anyone to feel sorry for me, either.

Tony must be killing himself laughing.

It's hard to speak with half a biscuit lodged in your mouth when you can't eat it or spit it out.

I manage to say through the crumbs, 'Is that what everybody says? Is everybody going around saying they feel sorry for me?'

Tony must think I'm the classic example of a self-made, fatal double bind.

'What the hell do you think?' says Fletcher.

He throws himself back down on the grass. I hear the *thwack* of his head as it hits the turf. He doesn't say 'ouch'.

I know he's right. I've seen it in everybody's eyes, and I have not seen it – because I did/didn't want to see it. But everybody *is* sorry for me. Everybody *knows* I'm going to die.

'Then why don't they do something?' I mumble. 'Why don't they stop me from dying?'

'Hello?' says Fletcher. 'What do you think I've been trying to do? Why do you think I've lodged half a stupid biscuit in your stupid half-open mouth?'

I flinch.

'You have all of life stretching in front of you, and you want to throw it away. All of this.' Fletcher points at the honeysuckle, at the tree overhead, the grass cuttings. 'Everything is yours. All you have to goddamn do is swallow an effing biscuit. But you won't, will you?' He laughs a hoarse laugh. 'No, you won't swallow the biscuit, and you're happy to see me die trying to make you. That's how selfish you are, Dani.'

I know he's right, but he doesn't understand about the points, and the panic and the Alien and the flooding. He doesn't understand that I might drown the world. That I have to stop myself. He doesn't understand that when I try to live, everything flips up on me, and I'm swallowed into a black hole. He doesn't understand how cold it is in Outer Space. He just doesn't understand.

And neither do I.

Tears are running down my face. I'm not sobbing. It's so hard trying to stay alive. Such a balancing act. And I wish I were dead. Maybe. And I say so.

'No, you don't,' says Fletcher. 'Don't say that. Not after everything I've done for you. I can't believe that. I think you're going to die, and I think you're making yourself die, but I don't think you wish it. Not truly. If I thought that, I'd walk away right now.'

I take hold of his hand. He can't leave me. I won't allow it.

'I can't save you,' says Fletcher sadly. 'I wish I could. I think I would do almost anything to save you. And I know you're doing all this because you think nobody loves you. But I love you, Dani. Although I know you won't believe that. Maybe you can't believe you're lovable in any way. But that's all I can do: just love you.' He raises himself up on to one elbow. He takes the half biscuit from my mouth and throws it into the bushes.

It is such a simple, kind gesture, filled with such despair.

I tremble. Can't stop.

And then he leans down. For a moment, I think he's going to kiss me again. He's trembling too and his breath is cold.

I tense up. He feels it.

'I'm in love with you,' he says softly.

He pulls back.

'And I can't save you.'

'Fletcher,' I say.

'And I can't bear it.'

'Please?'

'I am,' he says. He strokes the back of my hand. His eyes are alight with a gentle glow. 'I'm in love with you, and I'm not going to lie about it. I'm in love with you, and if you are determined to die, then I must accept it. I surrender. I have found my Higher Power. I am in love with you.'

'Fletcher,' I say again.

I'm drowning in a terrifying happiness. I can't tell him I love him back. I don't want to give him my hopeless, blighted, conditional love. He deserves so much more.

I look at him and let him look at me, until he turns away and stares up at the sky.

STEP SEVEN
SHORTCOMINGS

38

Tomorrow is here.

Nothing is making sense.

Fletcher hasn't come to Circle Time.

I keep hoping the door will open, and he'll stumble in. Or that he will message me that he's in the library, on the case again. I want to see that soft glow in his eyes. Hear more about his Higher Power. I try telling myself, *It's not my fault.* If I could have, I'd have swallowed that biscuit. We can't save anybody else. We can only save ourselves. This is his choice. He's choosing not to come to Circle Time. It probably is my fault. He's choosing to get thrown out of the programme. He really has given up. I should have swallowed that biscuit. Perhaps he wants to come to Circle Time, but is feeling too bad. It's his decision. If I'd tried harder, I'd have been able to swallow. He said he's in love with me. He's choosing not to see me. He can't bear to see me. I am going to die. The thoughts spiral in my head.

Tony is telling his life history. We have to do Tony's life

history once a week. That is, unless they can get a guest speaker to come and tell us their life history. Today we listen to Tony again.

'My name is Tony, and I am an addict. It bowls me over that here I am, an addict, with more years inside prison than you guys have lived and here I am talking to you. This can only happen in very special groups. This kind of love only happens in recovery. I didn't know what the heck I wanted when I was an addict. I couldn't say I needed love. I couldn't say that I needed to give love. I need to say it now: I really want to be loved. I blossom on love and I want to give love to all of you. You know, addicts are the best people. We are unbelievably kind, unbelievably real, unbelievably friendly, unbelievably slippery and unbelievably deceitful too. But above all we're indescribably intelligent. Yes, we run strategies, don't we?

'Anyway, back in the day, when I went to school, they brought in professionals who said: DON'T SMOKE. Don't smoke cigarettes and certainly don't smoke weed. Because if you start on weed you'll end up smoking crack. It was known as the Gate-way Drug Theory.'

I glance across at Lee. He grins back at me, raises one eyebrow and points at himself, like he's saying: Yup, that's right. Unbelievably kind, unbelievably real, unbelievably friendly, totally conniving and fabulously intelligent and on the hard stuff. That's me!

There's something about Lee that's irrepressible. I can see why Fletcher defends him.

Tony's voice drops a notch. 'They didn't know in those

171

days that addiction is a disease and that the development of the disease follows certain patterns. The thing was, I was sitting there, listening to those experts, thinking: *OMG how exciting. That sounds like an adventure that'll take me far away, away from this shithole I'm living in*, while the other kids in class were thinking: *Holy shit, that sounds dangerous. I better not do that.*

'But that's us. We are addicts. We're a special club. Still, thank heaven I shot so much heroin. Thank heaven I smoked so much crack, because I've broken through and found a world I never knew existed: a world where nobody else gets to make me different from who I am. A world that has introduced me to all of you, sitting here, and to the freedom that recovery can bring.'

I like Tony. There's something all right about him. He's only fake because he has to be. He doesn't try to hide it, either. Every line on his face tells me he's sorry about having to shoot crap at us.

'Well, the first time I started to use, it wasn't anything too serious. I just found my dad's whisky bottle. I used to have to hold my nose to drink it. But I wasn't drinking it for the taste – I was drinking it for the high. That's what made me different from most of the other mortals down here on Planet Earth. They didn't need to get high in order to feel human. That's what makes us addicts special, makes us star-crossed beings. I just wanted to get high, higher than the stars, get way up there, back towards my celestial home – and I wasn't fussy about what got me there either.'

Vaguely, I wonder if Tony has an Alien? It's a new and

disturbing thought. Maybe all addicts have aliens? Maybe Tony has my Alien. I frown. I don't want to share my Alien with him.

Tony pauses, seems to look at me as if he understands. 'And you know why? Because until I got into recovery, I felt like an outsider. I was never going to belong. Not even to myself. I felt that inside me was a big, bottomless black hole.' He looks at me again. 'Then one day, I saw little rows of white powder, lined up on a table and that's when I discovered my true love: heroin.'

Tony's voice breaks, grows hoarse. 'And, wow, I broke every rule in my book. I swore I would not become a thief – well, that was the first one to go. I swore I would not become a prostitute, but soon I was living on the streets, selling my arse to whoever wanted it. I just didn't care what I did, as long as I could use. That was how little I thought of myself.

'Yep, I did pretty much anything for that otherworldly buzz. I tried everything to see if it could fill the void inside me. You know how when you cheat at crosswords and you choose a word you know doesn't really fit, and you write it into the spaces and try to change the other words around it? Well, that was me. I tried filling up the emptiness inside me with anything I could lay my hands on. I tried blaming the world around me. But that hole can only truly be filled up by recovery, by a twelve-step programme.'

Jennifer is staring right at me. Like she's jealous that Tony glanced in my direction. Like she's already much further on the road to recovery than I am. Like she's totally on Step Twelve now and is doing well. Sometimes I hate Jennifer. I really can't see her as a star-crossed being. I hate her stupid haircut. Everything about her shouts out: YOU MUST APPROVE OF ME. YOU MUST SEE THAT I AM SO MUCH BETTER THAN YOU.

Tony hasn't finished, but he is winding down. 'I don't even know how I got to the point I did. How my disease got so bad. How it was ever going to stop. Then I got involved with a twelve-step programme. I started walking the path to recovery. Really, it's very simple. And this is it: first you must accept you have lost your way. Then you must allow The Twelve Steps to guide you. You start following their map. You find a way through all the shit. Until you hit the light. The journey is long, and before you can settle into recovering for ever, you have to find somebody else who is lost and hand the map on to them. It's really that simple. The lost get found. The sick get healed. And that's how tender and kind the programme is.'

39

Tony is done with his life history. He's now on to reviewing the Steps.

'The First Step is about honesty. I'm not talking about the kind of honesty which means that when you find a five-pound note you hand it in. It's when you say, "I'm going to stop using tomorrow." You gotta come clean. No more lying. You have to knock it off. BE HONEST. Got it?

'Then the Second Step is about your Higher Power. It's about your Belief System. Perhaps you have issues with the word "God". You might think, *Oh, yeah, that God, the one who got me into this shit to begin with. The one who rules over this messed-up planet.* But it's not about that.

'It's like when you sit out on the grass with a friend, feeling warm and comfortable, or when you read a good book that's totally gripping. You see, it's about something outside of yourself that gives you the strength to feel good about yourself. That's what the Higher Power is. It just means you're not the whole blasted centre of your entire blasted universe.'

We're halfway through CT, and still no Fletcher.

I don't know if I can make it to the end. I want to get up and rush out of the room, race up the stairs, kick his door open, shake him, slap him, punch, scratch, scream, knock some sense into him. I want to shout to his face, 'YOU CAN'T DO THIS.'

But I don't.

Instead, I listen to Atticus, who's sharing his encounter with the Second Step. Right now in his story he has shot so much heroin into himself, he doesn't care about anything. He's back there, anchored in his story. He's as high as a kite on his own memory. There are two spots of colour on his cheeks. And his eyeballs are rolled upwards.

What is Fletcher thinking of?

Is he mad?

Is this his last stand?

The ultimate Dani guilt trip?

It's a cry for help. Isn't it always? A siren from a distant galaxy saying SOS. But even if I go to him now, and I force myself to ram a three-course meal inside my poor shrunken stomach, it'll be no good. Fletcher has gone too far. I know. I saw that emptiness in his eyes. I felt a thousand antennae stretching and waving around out there in Outer Space. Aliens are like that. They're like vultures that instinctively circle when you're dying. They can smell despair.

At long last, Atticus shuts up.

Tony passes round the aphorisms card.

And the session ends.

We all stand and chant the Serenity Prayer. We join hands and pump out together how we're going to work it because we're worth it.

Only I am not worth it.

And Fletcher *is* worth it.

I run from the room.

Immediately I feel dizzy. I have to stop at the stairwell. With one hand I grasp hold of Carmen's foot and with the other the old wooden banisters. Steady.

'Sorry,' I say.

The smooth wood slips beneath the palms of my hand. Carmen's foot is still damp. I stagger across to the wall and bend over an old cast-iron radiator. Its chill touch refreshes. I press my cheek against the cold iron.

'Easy does it,' she says. 'This too will pass.'

I look up at her. She smiles down at me and winks one eye from her canted-over head.

'My neck is broken,' she says. 'In case you're wondering why I'm winking like this.'

I'm not sure I can get up the stairs. All the male state-funded clients have their rooms on the far end of the fifth floor. I am so weak. In the attics. Beyond the library. That's ten sets of stairs. I have to see Fletcher. It's where they store the stuff that's unmended or no longer needed. I have to see him now. Iggy used to joke about that. Fletcher has to go and talk to Tony right now. Joke about how we were the attic-dwellers, the flotsam of mankind. If Fletcher can catch Tony while he's still in the meeting room perhaps he can just be put down as a late, not as a no-show. Tony likes him.

Attics that still house the discarded, broken lumber of society.

I look up the staircase. My breathing is shallow. My heartbeat rapid. I feel dizzy. A jelly-like numbness has spread down my legs.

I pass the next landing.

The Alien sits on the landing above me.

'I can help,' it says.

It reaches down one long, electric-blue tentacle and gently wraps it around my waist. I can't fight the Alien any more.

'OK,' I whisper. And I let it haul me up the last few steps.

Sometimes you have to accept whatever help you can. Even if it means defeat.

'You really can't manage without me,' smirks the Alien. 'However hard you try.'

On the landing I stop to catch my breath. I bend over another old, cold radiator. My heart isn't beating in any regular way. It runs patterns. It plays out a frantic offbeat rhythm. Weak heartbeats softly punch my chest. For one terrible minute, I think I'm going to have some sort of seizure.

I try to remember the days when I ran up and down the school staircase, six times every break; how I pretended I'd left a pencil at the top, or my bag at the bottom. How nobody ever suspected.

I look at the next flight of stairs. They seem to stretch for ever in front of me, every step as difficult as the North Face of Everest. And the Alien is there again. So I rest on the stairs where the shadow of Carmen is at its darkest, and my heart beats and skips.

I lean on the radiator again, but now its coldness is not refreshing. Its icy touch is reaching into my mind. I feel a freezing sweat break out on my forehead. It travels round the crown of my head in a circlet of ice, down the centre of my spine, through the marrow of each rib, until it forms an ice cave over my heart.

I hear voices. Someone is shouting. It's coming from way above me. I don't mean to listen. I have no choice.

It's coming from way above Carmen's landing.

'You just don't understand, do you?' It's Tony.

'I understand everything.' Fletcher's voice. I vaguely wonder how Tony got up to Fletcher's room before me.

'No, you don't,' says Tony. 'You don't understand without recovery there is no future for you, Fletcher. You've been out there on the streets before – you know it's a one-way road to hell.'

'I'm not going out there to look for a future,' says Fletcher. 'I'm trying to lose one.'

'I did mental hospital, jail, years inside; I nearly smoked and drank myself into the grave. You know what the streets have to offer better than anyone here.' Tony's Scouse accent is thick with anger.

There's a thumping going on.

'Do you know how hard I have to fight to get these places funded for people like you and Lee?' screams Tony. He sounds more like Fletcher's dad than his therapist.

'Can we leave Lee out of this?' says Fletcher.

Except Fletcher never had a dad.

'Do you know how many benevolent, patronizing bastards

I have to grovel to?' shouts Tony. 'Do you know how many times I've got to show them the scars of my track marks just to get them to listen? How I have to sick up my past and go over and over and over my humiliation so that they'll sign the cheques that let you be here? Do you know all that?'

There's a silence.

Fletcher says, 'I didn't ask you to.'

'Oh great,' says Tony. 'Is that what you've learned after all the hours I've sat with you? To spit my own words back at me? What you don't understand, Fletcher, is that I will go on doing it. I'll go on licking arse and being the ignorant, unedu-cated, jailbird moron, and dancing my flappy, little, sickening dance in front of Big Money – and I will do it for a thousand years. I will do it until I drop dead. Why? Because I don't want another underprivileged, undervalued by this effing Capitalist stupid system, misguided, trauma-damaged, annoying, heartbroken, diseased young man to do what I had to do in order to survive.'

There's a pause.

'Do you think, when I go and tell my life history at Circle Time, that's the real story?' There's a break in Tony's voice. 'I've seen you looking at me, Fletcher. I know you know the truth. I haven't fooled you. I know you see right through me. You understand how much I've cleaned up everything.'

There is a pause. I hear a gulping sound.

Tony's voice is completely broken now. 'You're like my own kid, Fletch. Yeah, the one that won't talk to me any more. *And I want to save you.* I know it shouldn't be like that – I shouldn't make any personal investment in you, you've got to do it for yourself. But I see something in you, Fletcher. I see that you can be OK – you can heal, you really can. You can recover and it totally breaks me to see you throwing it away.'

There's a very long pause.

'So you think about it.' The crack in his voice is still there: straight from the back of his throat down to the shadow of Carmen. 'Just effing think about it.'

The door on the landing above slams. Someone stamps on to the floorboards. I hear a punching noise and bits of plaster land around me. I press myself against the wall. There's the fast beat of footfall. They crash down the wooden stairway. They reach the landing and come round it.

And I see Tony, red-faced, bleary-eyed. He pauses, draws the back of his hand across his nose and stares at me.

'I hope you're effing happy now,' he mutters. There is a salty, blaming bitterness in his voice, unlike anything I've ever heard from him before.

I press myself back against the wall. I want to dissolve. I want to erase myself. I want all this to stop. I want to scream, 'THIS HAS TO STOP.' I can't stand it any more. I can't swallow. I try positive talk. Affirmations. *I am awesome. I am trying. I am lovable. I am loved. I am kind. I am truthful. I am trustworthy. I am kind.*

I press the tips of my fingers over my eyebrows. I try to take myself into a semi-hypnotic state. I repeat: *I am happy. I am happy. I am fulfilled. I am fulfilled. I am happy. I am happy. I am happy.*

I remove my fingertips. I can't stop the negative talk. It creeps back, like weeds in a garden. Strangling.

You're nothing. You're useless. You're cruel. You could have eaten that biscuit. This is your fault. You're evil. No wonder your mother tried to kill you. Fletcher will leave. You've broken Tony's heart. He will use on the streets and die, and it's your fault. It's all your fault.

The sunlight streams in through the landing window. It catches the side of the stairs. It falls short of catching me.

I stand in the shadows. I hear Tony's crunching step turn on the next landing, continue on down the stairs, kick open the swing doors at the bottom. I hear them slam shut. The footsteps fade.

I am alone on the landing in the shadows.

The ray of sunlight flickers. I look at the stairs ahead of me. I must climb them. I must find a way to put things right. It feels like I am standing on an empty shore on a tiny island.

I climb the stairs. No breath. No muscles left to pull me forward. I have to.

I reach the next landing and hang on to the balcony. I feel weak. I think I'm going to collapse. My heartbeat fades in and out, and stops and patters.

Step by step.

Just the next step.

I start to count them.

Step One: accept you are powerless.

Step Two: believe in your Higher Power.

The wood of the banister is hard and the palms of my hands sweaty.

I make it to the next landing. A finger of sunlight has crept through the blinds and is lighting a stripe of lemon-yellow up the staircase ahead of me. It touches the bottom of Fletcher's door.

I want to call out. I want him to open up and bounce down the stairs and, with all the strength of those amazing shoulders, pick me up and carry me up the next flight and into his room.

I imagine his arms cradling me. But I can't cry out.

On what basis can I call to him now? It's my turn to help him.

On the third stair, I sit and rest. The sweat on my palms, my wrists, is sticky on my forehead.

Seconds tick. The sound of an aeroplane far away grows louder, passes, dies out. And behind the silence that the aircraft leaves in its wake, a great, unheard stillness seems to be bulging down, pressing into the jet stream of the plane.

I think of coming into existence, budding, blossoming, fruiting, changing, fading, dying. I hear the great silence of the before and the after. What does it all mean anyway, this little life? This irregular beating heart, these sweaty palms? What is it all for?

And who cares?

Except that it won't go away.

My heartbeat comes back, tries to beat in a regular pattern again. My armpits sweat. My breathing continues even when I try to hold it. I can't hold it. Life will not be dismissed. It will not.

And the finger of light is still lying up the stairs, pointing the way to Fletcher's room. And I realize suddenly I want to walk in the light. I am tired of the cold of Outer Space. I'm tired of its darkness. I want to go into the light and feel its heat. I don't want some goddamn parasitic, Alien planet.

I crawl up the steps, and sit and lean my forehead against Fletcher's door.

40

Fletcher hears me. He swings the door open. I nearly fall in. He stands there. I can feel tornadoes of energy whirling around him.

'So you've come to shout at me too?'

It starts.

I smile. A tiny, wry smile. I wish. I wish I had the energy to shout. If I had the energy to shout, I'd blast him with a hurricane of words. I'd send a torrent of vocabulary all over him; he would gasp for breath and try to swim in its flood.

'Just help me into your room,' I say.

He picks me up. I feel the power of his shoulders. He places me on his bed. It's unmade. It smells of boy. I don't care. I want to find the plughole to the ocean of words. I want to drown him with them; drown together.

'Well?' he says.

'Stop it.'

'You started this,' he says.

'I'm sorry,' I say. It's probably the hardest thing I've ever said, and I am not sorry for my Thinness. My Thinness has been my friend. It has seen me through the years. When Fletcher is thrown out of rehab, my Thinness will be there to comfort me. How can I be sorry about that? But I am. I truly am.

'So you can stop it?' he says.

I take in tiny breaths. Everything in me wants to shout out, blame him, to say: Why didn't you come to Circle Time? You're punishing me? Do you want to fail the programme? *Do you love being a crackhead that much?* All that finding and searching and promising to be there for me, all of it just rubbish?

'What do I have to do to stop it?' I say.

He sighs. And in his eyes there's something so massive that I'm afraid.

'You could have chased up your mate and found out more about your past.'

'I did.'

'But nothing came of it. It was all just me, trying to fix you.'

'I want to be fixed,' I say. 'I just don't know how to do it.'

'The answer to that is simple,' he says. 'You eat.'

I laugh at that. If only the answer was so simple. If that was all it took, I would not even be sitting here now.

And Fletcher knows that. In that massive hole in his eyes, I can see that he understands about the Thinness and the Alien and the need for a loving mother; understands about the body and me and the love that never existed; and the desolate landscape where you sit alone and the wind blows and you're so cold and tired and it never stops, even though you think you're crying out loud for help, 'For God's sake, somebody must understand, somebody must rescue me. Isn't there somebody out there who's in charge of all this?'

But there isn't anybody in charge.

No knight in shining armour.

I've placed all my power outside myself, into the hands of the cold empty universe, where only one opportunist Alien has noticed.

Simply having a meal would be delicious and wonderful, and I ache for it. Oh, to sit down – even on this unmade and stinky boy bed – and bite into a sandwich with the full-bloodedness of the hunger that has been raging inside me for over a decade. To bite down on tomato and bacon and butter and bread. I long for it. I dream of it.

But until I can get my ten points I'm not allowed to have any of it: no happiness, no food, no love.

I've been working so hard. Every day. I can't just cheat now and pick the sandwich up, can I?

I search for an answer in Fletcher's eyes.

What would that mean about all the other days, when I arrived first at every mealtime and ate nothing until the last person left? When I didn't even dare to have one leftover crust on somebody's plate though I longed for it?

He knows the answer is not so simple. 'Just let all that go,' says Fletcher. 'Kiss it goodbye. It's always the same – over and over.'

And I realize he's right. I'm obsessing and going over and

over the same thoughts, rolling myself tight into every double bind I can find. And I never get any further.

'And oh dear, I don't frankly give a damn.' Fletcher puts on a Southern drawl. 'It's all over.'

All over?

'It's not up to me to care about your games or your strategies or your points or anything any more.'

What does he mean?

He pulls out his smartphone. He puts it into selfie mode and pushes it into my face. 'Look at yourself. You're dying. I'm surprised you didn't die on the stairs out there. I love you, but if you've crawled up here to save me, you've wasted your energy. I can't help me. You can't help me. You can't even help yourself.'

'I'll eat then,' I say. 'I want you to stay, Fletcher. I don't want you to leave. I'm scared of being alone.'

It's the first time I've said that. And I ache with the acknowledgement of it.

I'm afraid of being alone.

I'm afraid of the Alien.

I'm terrified of the Thinness.

And if Fletcher goes, I don't know how I can continue to fight them.

Because even though I run the strategies, I have been fighting them. I always fight them.

'You don't understand, do you?' says Fletcher. 'I've accepted that being in love with you is my Higher Power. I accept that you'll do as you please, so it's not up to me to care any more whether you eat or not. But it goddamn hurts, so all I think about now is getting back on to the streets and finding the bus.'

'Please,' I say.

'The bus back to Cracksville.'

'I'll do it,' I say. 'I'll eat something.'

'I can't keep changing my mind just because you say you'll do this or do that. That's not how accepting a Higher Power works.'

Fletcher goes down on his knees and routs around under the bed. He drags out an old plastic Sainsbury's bag. The bag is torn and dusty and looks like it's been there a while.

'Plus I think it's gone too far, Dani. I don't think you can help yourself any more. Let's do a replay of the compost garden scene so you understand what I mean.'

He tips the contents on to the bed. Crumbs and bits of plastic and dirt spill out along with a half-opened pack of crisps.

I can tell at once that he didn't finish eating the crisps because he didn't like them. They're cheap, fake crisps in a cheap, fake packet and they're flavourless and have lost their crunch.

They probably never had any crunch.

Fletcher rips the pack fully open, tips the crisps on to the bed.

'All yours,' he says.

I know this is it.

I must eat the crisps.

It has come to this.

There is no other way. Because I do understand. Somehow I just didn't think it would end with a dusty pack of budget cheese and crunch-less onion. I can hear the Thinness laughing at me. All the meals I've refused. All the cupcakes with coloured cream toppings. All the plates of steaming vegetables, the pizza slices, the roast chicken.

To end it all with crumbled, old bits of crisps.

Fletcher watches me closely. He seems to be looking for something, some reaction.

'You understand, now, how hopeless it all is?' he says.

He's doing this to show me how powerless we both are. In a weird way I'm enjoying it though.

It shows he still cares.

I'm still the centre of his universe.

Fletcher's voice rises an octave. 'You see, you just crawled up here to show me how thin you are. I get it. You still want sympathy. "Look at me. I'm so thin. I'm dying. You must notice me. Don't leave me, Fletch. Stay and watch me die." You can't help yourself. It's all gone too far, Dani. And I can't take it.'

I pick up a crisp. It smells stale. My stomach heaves. My tongue feels dry. It's such a momentous task that I wonder if it's even possible for me to open my mouth. But I must open my mouth. I must. I slide the crisp between my lips. It sticks out. I try to draw it in further. I try to chew.

Fletcher sinks back on to the chair opposite. His eyes follow my every move.

It has all come down to this: one stale bit of crisp.

My chest trembles.

'It's a deal now, isn't it?' I croak. The crisp is still stuck to my lip. I could still spit it out. 'You'll go back to Circle Time?'

'The time for deals is over,' says Fletcher.

'I won't swallow it unless there's a deal,' I say.

'You're incredible,' he says. 'You won't swallow it unless I make a deal with you? Is that it? What's changed, Dani? Nothing. Absolutely nothing. You've blackmailed me with your goddamn thinness for the last time ever.' There's a break in his voice. 'I don't believe that you can swallow it even if you want to.'

My eyes start to water. Maybe it has all gone too far.

'I wanted you to get well so much,' he says, 'but you won't. You're determined to kill yourself. You want to die. You're just like my mum. I begged her to stop drinking. I cried. I hid the bottles. I took her credit card. I cut it into pieces. I threw it in the bin. I went to the corner shops, the booze stores, the pubs; I said, "Please don't sell alcohol to my mum." But it didn't make any difference. It just made her angry. That just made her drink more. And now you come crawling up the stairs to blackmail me with your thinness. I'm hurting too, Dani. I just can't show you bones and skin as proof . . .' He seems to gulp. He lifts up his chin. The muscles on the side of his face flex. 'Nothing I do makes any difference.'

And he's right. Nothing either of us does makes any difference. I have no power left to force deals on him. All the power I'd hoped to gain, all the control over what I eat or don't eat, is gone.

And I am truly powerless.

Just when I've found something I want more than the Thinness.

And I understand what I have to do.

I want to stop Fletcher from leaving me. So I open my mouth. I must place crisps properly inside my mouth. I must masticate. I must carry on masticating until I have a bolus of food and I must swallow it. And then maybe we can strike a deal. Maybe I can prove him wrong. Then maybe he'll stay.

My mouth is dry as sand, so I say, 'Can you get me a glass of water then?'

Fletcher hesitates, as if a glass of water wasn't part of the deal. Then he crosses the room to the little sink and removes his toothbrush from a none-too-clean tumbler, half fills it with water and offers it to me.

'It's no good, Dani,' he says. 'You can't save me any more than I can save you.'

And I can see that his hand is trembling and the surface of the water is rippling, and I take the glass because I can't turn the crisp into a bolus of food or swallow anything without some moisture, and I have none of my own left.

'Please don't watch,' I say.

'You haven't got a hope in hell of stopping me watching you,' says Fletcher. 'Don't think I haven't studied you during your supervised eating times and seen how you push bits of food around, drop them on the floor, hide them behind things or under the side of your plate – you even pick them up in your fingers, pretending to eat but start smoothing them into your hair instead. Just let it go, Dani. We're past all that.'

So this is it.

I place another crisp through my teeth and on to my tongue. I crumble off half of it. I raise the glass of water to my lips. I take a sip and let the water soak into the dryness inside my mouth. It feels like I've put the Alien in there.

I try to chew, but I can't manage the water and the food in my mouth at the same time. My tongue has forgotten how to roll and push it all around. I gently shove the waterlogged crisp against my teeth and crush it. A dribble of water spills on to my chin. My taste buds flare up, like beacons. Something inside my chest quivers. It's only dirty, stale bits of crisps, but my body is crying out for them, and I can feel its longing. My eyes well up with tears. I don't know if I want to cry with happiness now that I'm allowing myself to eat something, or howl with self-pity now that I'm forcing myself to break my own life-saving strategies.

'Look,' says Fletcher. 'Spit it out. I'm sorry for everything. It's OK.'

He's trying to say: Death is easier than watching you trying to live.

But I want to live. I want Fletcher to live too.

So I work my throat. I try to push the melting crisp-mush back towards my epiglottis but it closes up. I try again. It won't open. I think I'm going to gag. I glance at Fletcher. He's still watching, of course. I raise the glass of water to my lips and take another sip. I lift my chin up. I let the water trickle back through my mouth till it's there at the very neck of my throat with the sogginess, and I can't breathe and I struggle for air, and in desperation my throat opens and I swallow.

'Oh, Dani,' says Fletcher.

There's no 'well done', no stroking my hand; there's no praising, no coaxing.

Why should there be? I'm only doing what most people do all the time.

Do I expect praise for breathing?

I'll prove it to him. I will eat. Then he can go back to Circle Time.

It's my own deal with myself.

My hand picks up another bit of crisp. This time I know what to do. This time it should be easier. But it's not. It's as if the Alien has stationed itself over my throat now. All its tentacles are sentry men. Having allowed one bit of food through, it has raised the drawbridge. Nothing may pass this way again.

I get an overwhelming urge to rush to the sink and gag, to spit out anything that's left in my mouth. I can't rush anywhere. I'm too weak.

'Stop it,' says Fletcher.

I squash the last bits of crisp into crumbs and roll them across my lips. They all spill back out on to the bed.

'For God's sake, Dani, stop it,' says Fletcher.

He scoops dirt and crumbled crisp bits off the duvet and throws them into the bin.

And something inside me cracks.

I drag the bin over to the bed. I scrabble around inside. I will do it. I find bits of crisp and dust and tissue. I roll them into a ball. I open my mouth. I will do it. I will save us.

I have to do it.

I WILL EAT. I WILL EAT.

I put the ball of rubbish in my mouth. But I can't. I can't. I can't save myself.

'I will eat,' I scream, 'and I want a deal.'

'The deal was that there is no deal,' says Fletcher.

'But I want one,' I say.

I feel sick. I feel out of control. My hand is shaking. The water spills on the bed.

'We don't have any goddamn deal any more,' says Fletcher.

'You said you wanted all this to stop,' I say. 'You said it was simple. Just eat – that's what you said. I tried as hard as I could. You said that would make it all stop.'

'You're getting hysterical,' says Fletcher. 'And you're trying to bully me.'

'It's not fair. I really tried hard. We had a deal.'

Fletcher shakes his head. 'I said it's all over, Dani. It's gone too far.'

Something inside me is torn apart.

The Alien is back. He's grown six metres tall. He's covered in livid red streaks. He stretches his tentacles out around every wall and places his suckers on them. He shakes the room.

It's all Fletcher's fault. He doesn't have to leave.

The ceiling cracks. Great chunks of plaster fall and hit the bed and mix with the crumbs of crisps.

'IT'S NOT FAIR,' I scream.

'It's not fair?' Fletcher says. 'Do you think it's fair to stand by and watch someone die? Do you think that's fair?'

'You're doing it too,' I say. 'If you go back on the streets then you're doing the same thing.'

'How do you know what I'll be doing? You don't know anything about the streets. You don't know the life I've led. You don't know where I'll go. I'll just walk out of here and that will be the end of it for you.'

195

'Don't lie to yourself,' I say. 'You're going back out there to use. You know you are.'

'So now you're goddamn clairvoyant,' he says.

I want to shake him. I want to explode. I want the Alien to devour him.

'I don't need to be clairvoyant. You are a crackhead,' I say. I'm so mad at myself. 'You have no control. Even Lee is better than you – at least he doesn't pretend he's trying to get well.'

'Leave. Lee. Alone,' Fletcher mutters between clenched teeth.

'You've never tried to get well.' The floodgates are washed away. I'm going to drown him now. 'You don't care about recovery. You just want to invest every last bit of energy in every person you meet, and then you can play Mr Big Hero, Mr Save the Goddamn World, and look BIG in front of everyone, while you don't confront any of your own problems. That's it. It's just you having a big wank in front of everyone and we're all supposed to cheer you on.'

The Alien is doing a dance, something between a tango and rock 'n' roll. The room is shaking, more plaster crashes down on to the floor. The boards begin to buckle under the bed.

Fletcher kicks the plaster away. He throws the chandelier that has fallen on him at the Alien. He picks up the bin and empties the rest of it out of the window. A new black hole forms in Andromeda.

'You only ate that bit of crisp and did all that drama with the bin because you want to get your own way,' Fletcher says. 'Because you want me to stay and watch you die. Because you're terrified of being alone. Because if I leave this programme you'll be alone. You won't have anyone to text. You won't have anyone to kneel at your feet and worship you and beg you to stop killing yourself. You won't have anyone at all, except your goddamn Alien.'

The Alien stops shaking the room, withdraws all its tentacles, reduces its antennae to little fluffy ears. It shrinks itself into a kittenish ball and blinks wide eyes at me, rolls to my feet and snuggles between my ankles.

'You can keep your goddamn Alien,' says Fletcher. 'You could've had me – all of me. We could've been a team. I thought we were a team. I thought we were going to recover together. I thought we were going to fight this thing. I spent hours lying on my bed at night, visualizing the future, willing it to happen. You and me, in some goddamn cheap rented bedsit, waking up clean and sober, just recovering and going to our addiction groups and staying recovered. I didn't want mansions and gardens and fast cars. I just wanted to wake up with you, sober and recovered.'

The Alien reforms itself into a caterpillar and crawls on to my lap. Somewhere in Outer Space the black hole widens and galaxies disappear.

11

A rented bedsit and waking up in Fletcher's arms, whole and recovered and loved.

The thought has electricity about it.

Eight hundred kilovolts of pure bliss.

Eight hundred kilovolts of pure terror.

I wrap my arms around my Thinness so he won't see me trembling.

'No, you don't want that, do you?' Fletcher's voice is hoarse. He leans over me, watching my face, like a cat watching a mouse hole. 'You're just keeping me happy – anything to keep me kneeling in front of you – and you call that real? I'd rather have all the fakery in the goddamn universe than that. I'd rather be on the streets because . . . because inside you is nothing – nothing for me.' Fletcher turns his face away, leans over the small handbasin and grips its sides. 'No love.' He slumps his shoulders. 'You're cold, Dani. Cold as Outer Space.'

The Alien won't stand for that.

It turns into a spitting cobra, slithers to the end of the bed, rears up, thrusts its head back and sprays Fletcher with venom.

No love inside me. Nothing.

'And you know all about manipulation, don't you?' I say. I can't stop the acid seeping into my voice.

As empty as the empty room.

'You. The state-funded crackhead. The voice of righteousness. The man of the streets. The hero of a thousand crack dens. Oh, let me bow down at the shrine of Fletcher.'

And that's the thing when you're wounded. You wound back. Any way you can. Even with blunt-edged words that hardly make sense.

But it's not what you say.

It's the way you say it.

Fletcher turns, brings his head up, wipes the venom from his face and looks at me. The words have done their work.

I sip at his pain. I'm hungry for it. It's like when you put a piece of chocolate on your tongue. It takes you over and whilst you promised yourself it will only be one square, you find yourself reaching for the next, and the next, as you vow to vomit it all out – if only – if only you can continue to binge on its sweetness.

Hurt is written all over his face. And I can't help myself. I must hurt some more. Everything in me swells up. I choose the sharpest barb of all.

Wound him even more deeply.

'Yes, you.' My voice drops to a new toxic low. 'The boy who'd like to have an orchestra of violins playing when he tells us how he tried to save his poor, dear, darling, drunken

Sarah Mussi

mother. How he cried in the corner and hid her bottles of whisky. How he blamed himself for her death.'

I pause, then push the arrow home. 'YAWN.'

Like all addiction, now it has started it can't be stopped.

And the Alien spreads himself into a festival of rainbows and pours fountains of sparkling crystal water over everything and changes the drops into fireworks.

At least one of us is happy.

'You bitch,' yells Fletcher. 'You goddamn bitch. Who do you think you are? Look at you. Do you think *that* looks good?' He points at all my precious Thinness. 'Yeah, I've looked through your phone. I've seen all your Thinspo collection. You think *that* looks beautiful? You're fricking mental. Fricking, goddamn, ugly, fricking, mental skeleton.'

'SHUT UP, SHUT UP, SHUT UP.' I'm shouting now, loud enough to wake all the dead of Daisy Bank Rehab. Tony is going to come all the way back up the stairs and tell us we're both thrown out.

'Oh yeah?' sneers Fletcher. 'So I should "SHUT UP, SHUT UP, SHUT UP" because some goddamn lunatic pervert mother locked you up?'

That's it. I've had enough.

'Your mum was a psycho,' he hollers.

I know the best way to hurt.

'Just like you,' he shouts.

I know it.

This is my moment.

I rise to my feet. I'm surprised to find that I'm not at all shaky; I call the Alien to heel. I raise up my chin. I look

200

Fletcher in the eye. This is my crowning moment. I feel powerful. I feel awesome. I can deliver the death thrust.

And I do.

It's quite simple.

'Good,' I say. 'We understand each other. Goodbye and good luck with the rest of your sorry little life, Fletcher.'

I call to the Alien. It jumps into my arms like a loving puppy. I turn on my heel. I walk out of the door. I don't slam it, because I'm no longer emotionally engaged with him. I've just relocated myself. I'm floating out over the Milky Way into Outer Space. A gentle wind is rippling towards me from a humongous black hole. It's teasing out the strands of my hair. But I leave it behind. I close the door in a very respectable and ladylike way.

I leave him.

I leave the black hole to swallow him up.

Before I go to sleep I email Kerstin. I'm so furious at her. I want to blame her. If she'd bothered to help, this might never have happened. Fletcher might not have given up on me. I do blame her. She was supposed to be a friend.

Dear Kerstin,

 I guess you haven't been able to find out anything about my early history. I can't lie, I'm pretty disappointed. I don't know how to think about this. I really need that info. I explained to you that it's mega important. You said you'd do anything for me. I'm struggling with how that fits in with you not having done this – the one thing I asked for. Anyway, don't bother any more. It doesn't matter. Here in rehab we learn a bit about karma – what goes around comes around. LOL.

X Dani

FLIGHT THREE

WISDOM TO UNDERSTAND

STEP EIGHT
WILLING TO MAKE AMENDS

42

I wake up with the word 'pervert' going round and round inside my head.

There's something unwholesome yet addictive about it. I grasp it with the hands of my mind. It dances in front of my eyes, echoes in my ears. It's outlined in neon lights.

Fletcher has given up on me.

I get up. I walk to the little sink, reach for a glass and absent-mindedly pour myself a cup full of water.

Fletcher called me a bitch.

These days I've been rationing even water, in case it makes the scales go up. But this morning for some strange reason I don't care. I sit on the edge of the bed and look at the word 'pervert' as it dances in front of my eyes.

Fletcher said I was cold.

I sip the water.

And my mother was a pervert.

And suddenly it comes to me.

I cannot quite hold on to it.

Fletcher, I've remembered . . .

The glass slips from my hand, breaks, and water sprays cold on to my feet and legs.

There was a third person in the room.

The word 'pervert' makes me see him. *He* dances in front of my eyes. Huge, arms like tentacles. His footsteps echo in my ears. My insides dissolve. The smell of him. His face is outlined in neon lights.

And suddenly I'm back there . . .

I'm sitting on the floor with my eyes wide open, and the footsteps are coming, and my mother is trying to hold the door handle shut, which is strange because we're locked in, and she should be trying to open it.

I can't close my eyes because I know something terrible is going to happen.

My mother isn't strong enough to stop the door opening. She cries and falls. I hear her elbow; I hear her shoulder hit the floor.

And I see him walk into the room. Behind him is a soft luminous light. And the word 'pervert' dances around him and rolls itself into a ball and zooms straight, like a bullet, in between his eyes, straight into the face of the man standing in the doorway.

He steps into the room.

My mother crawls across the floor and holds his ankle.

'No, leave her alone,' she pleads. 'Don't touch her. Please, for the pity of God! Leave her alone.'

The man shakes her hand off. Kicks her in the face.

He steps towards me.

I wet myself.

43

My heart floods. My knees tremble. I brush the water off my legs.

For some reason I don't curl my Thinness into me and hug it close.

Instead, I systematically bend down and pick up the pieces of the glass. There are four large pieces and two smaller bits. Tenderly, I put them back together and balance the shards as best I can, until the glass still looks like itself, though shattered and broken.

I place it back on the shelf above the sink.

It looks whole. It pretends it isn't destroyed.

And the darkness falls away from me.

And I am walking in the light.

And a surge of power comes over me.

And I know a number of things, and some of them are dreadful and some of them are beautiful.

44

The man steps towards me.

My mother screams. Begs. Pleads. I cannot look when he turns. I hear the blows, the crack of her head against the wall. And I know that in the room there is a darkness, and the darkness suffocates us and swallows me up.

And the man is still stepping towards me.

And I realize I don't have to be there. I can escape into the darkness.

So I look across at my mother and I smile at her. Because she has tried to defend me. And she's hurting. And that means she loves me. And knowing that I am loved by her defeats all the darkness.

💣 ☠ 👎

And after the third person has done to me all that he can, and he has gone away, and the door is locked again, my mother drags herself up and picks up the bowl that he placed on the floor.

She crawls to my side and puts the food in front of me and holds me very tenderly and says, 'Oh, my poor baby, my poor baby.'

And I say, 'Did he hurt you, Mummy?'

And after some time she says, 'Will you eat?'

And I say, 'You eat too, Mummy?'

And she says, 'I'm not hungry.'

And I look at the food. So little. It is not enough for both of us.

'Please eat it, my darling,' she says. 'I'm really not very hungry at all, and I like being thin.'

And she is thin. I can feel her Thinness as she holds me. And I eat the food because I'm very hungry, but I know I ate the food yesterday and I ate the food the day before.

And I'm very sure that she must be very hungry too.

But she loves me, and her Thinness comforts me, so I eat all the food.

45

And the tendrils of the darkness withdraw and I step into the light.

And I know that I am loved, in the most powerful way, and I know that I am awesome and I know that nothing that happened in that room can steal that away from me.

And I know that I have been punishing myself ever since. Punishing myself for having eaten the food that my mother gave me.

Searching for her Thinness.

Starving her to death.

46

I'm so happy. I'm so excited. It feels like all the sunshine in the universe is pouring through me, that the blood in my veins is liquid heat. I must find Fletcher! I must tell him. I must explain why I've lived all these years in the darkness. Why I've done such dreadful things. I must thank him. I must tell him how that *one word* he dragged out of the black hole inside himself has freed me.

He will be so pleased.

He doesn't really mean it's over.

I can show him I'm not cold.

He wanted to help me and now he has.

I'm so excited; I think I might even eat something at breakfast. I don't need to get there first. I look at the broken glass delicately balanced together. It's broken but it's still whole! All the pieces are still there.

I get down to breakfast. I look at all the food on the self-service counter. I can eat! I can give myself permission to eat something today. My mother gave me food;

211

she wants me to eat. She wants me to eat the best things there are.

An apple winks at me from the top of a pile. It's rosy on one side, delicate yellow-green on the other, with the prettiest dapples. Today I will eat an apple. No longer forbidden fruit. This rosy, green, dappled apple will be the fruit of knowledge. Of self-knowledge!

Suddenly I'm waxing all metaphoric and poetic, and it's cheesy and it's probably all been said before, but it's not fake!

And it's not funny.

It's real.

I pick the apple off the pile. I cross to the table by the window. I sit and wait.

I don't eat it, because I want to share this moment with Fletcher.

I wait for Fletcher to join me.

Outside the sun is shining down across the lawn, across the stone steps, catching sparkles from the little fountain. Today is a new day. Today I can walk in the light *all day*. Today I can bite into an apple, feel the crisp skin break beneath my teeth. Feel the squirt of apple juice hit the roof of my mouth.

WITH NO STRATEGIES.

And Fletcher will be able to come back to Circle Time.

A shiver of pleasure contracts in my throat at the thought. My eyes actually start to water.

NO STRATEGIES.

I'm not looking for points.

I was loved.

I WAS LOVED.

And, now I come to think of it, even the Alien loved me. Though weirdly he isn't around now.

Oh, I just can't wait for Fletcher to come. I'm wanting him *so badly*. I want to say sorry. I want to tell him I can heal now. My body is singing to be alive. Singing to be near him. I can be there for him. We can make this work. We can start again. We can get that bedsit. We can get through each day being there for each other.

We really can make this work.

Fletcher does not come.

Perhaps he's mad at me. Of course he's mad at me. I was horrible to him yesterday. I said unforgivable things. His mother was a bitch. He needed me so badly. And my mother loved me. And he tried so hard to save me. And I locked him out. Of course he's mad at me. I reach for my phone.

After breakfast I'm going to find him. I'm going to make a true apology. I imagine going down on my knees. I don't care. I'm going to be very dramatic. I'll throw out my arms beseech-ingly.

No.

I banish that image from my head. I don't want to be affected or pretentious or manipulative. No more starring in my own movie. I just want to tell him how really, really, really, really, really sorry I am. How wrong I got it. How much we need each other. How important it is to try again. *How we can do it.* Just stick together. Just believe in each other.

But then Kerstin arrives.

One of the very helpful members of staff informs me she's waiting in the conservatory.

47

My heart sinks.

I'd forgotten about Kerstin.

I put the apple down. I leave the refectory.

Daisy Bank Rehab Centre encourages visitors. They encourage interaction with the Real World.

I walk down the corridor to the visitors' section.

I don't know why they call it the Real World. As if they have a monopoly on reality.

Ceramic tiles wink up at me.

If I refuse to visit with Kerstin it would be making a statement. A statement that would be noticed – especially by Judith.

It might involve hours of individual psychotherapy to help me understand why I'm isolating myself despite the fact that the Real World wants to reach out to me.

I sigh.

The wall clock chimes the hour. 9:00A.M.

I can make it quick. Maybe?

Kerstin is bound to be pissed off about the email. That's why she's come so early.

She's *furious*.

She's planning on annihilating me.

She's screaming for blood.

I can tell her something, then I can leave. Give her biscuits. Smile a lot, say, 'It's all my fault. Mood swings. My illness, you know? I'm sorry.' That usually works. Old lying patterns. I can't help it. *The last person I want to see is Kerstin.*

When I was so happy.

I push open the glass doors to the visitor's centre.

She's so manipulative.

She's *unreal*.

The place smells of floral disinfectant.

This is reality. It smacks you down.

Just when you've risen up.

I don't know why I even asked her to help me.

Everything about her is so faultless.

So fake.

If that is what the Real World is like.

They shouldn't call it the Real World.

48

I can see from the way Kerstin is sitting, smack in the middle of the wicker-cane sofa, that she is about to play death chess.

I used to play chess. I was quite good at it. It was the idea of running a strategy that appealed. It's always about power and control.

Any good chess manual will tell you that you must gain control of the centre of the board. Once you have control of the centre, you have control of the entire game.

Kerstin is sitting in the centre of the board, smack in the middle of the cane sofa, smack in the middle of the conservatory. She has purposely placed herself there. She isn't mucking about. She has come to kill. She has come to triumph. She's already countless moves ahead. And I can see that she has plenty of other gambits up her sleeve.

I must be careful.

I've given up strategies.

I will need protective armour.

I will run a sub-strategy.

216

I will put on my rubber diving suit.

I will follow Tony's advice.

Detach.

Observe. Don't absorb.

Watch what it's doing, follow every flicker of the eyebrow, every wave of the hand. Notice if it leans forward or falls back in its seat. Listen to the feeling behind its words. Breathe. Think how *you* feel.

Don't react.

Its words will be bullets aimed to kill.

Notice where the bullets are aimed: at your mind, your hair, your heart, your belly.

Zip fast your rubber suit, my darling baby; the bullets will bounce right off you.

Nothing can be absorbed through a rubber bodysuit.

I yank the zip tight. I pull the hood over my head. I put on my visor. And for good measure I plug a breathing tube into my mouth and link it up to an oxygen tank. And then I sit like a frogman in front of it.

'You look very pretty today.' It starts.

I do not look pretty. I'm wearing a frogman's diving suit – you can't even see anything of me. That bullet doesn't even need to be bounced off. It's totally wide of the mark.

I don't respond. I don't want to play this game with it.

'Hi, Dani.' It flutters a row of fingers at me; delicately manicured nails flash red.

I notice. It's warning me. There will be blood.

I wish I could go straight to Fletcher. He has never flashed red fingernails at me in this menacing way.

'Now, hmmm,' it says. 'I just had a chance to read through really carefully that email you sent me . . . Hmmm . . . '

I hate 'hmmm'. It's a cleverly reproachful, cleverly thoughtful, cleverly calculated, menacing put-down.

I take a sip of oxygen. That bullet nearly got me, right here at the side of my neck. I can feel the bruise.

'Darling, I was really upset by it. You seemed to be suggesting that I don't support your recovery because I've not rung people up and tried to find out things about that newspaper report.'

Here it comes! A rapid round of fire from a MAC-10. I mentally switch into *The Matrix* style and become the One. I warp and bend, and when I'm not quick enough and the bullet hits, I let the rubber absorb it, just enough to bounce it back. The words 'newspaper report' bounce off my heart and clatter loudly to the floor.

Oh, Fletcher. I did try. I really did.

'But you know that's utterly untrue! What you said was very mean and spiteful, and I'm deeply wounded by it.' It delivers this in a single spraying action and reloads the MAC-10.

I give it a silent handclap. Oh, brilliant – from 'suggesting' to 'saying' in a seamless transition with added insults.

What am I supposed to feel now? Sorry for her?

Be very careful. You slipped, Dani.

Feel sorry for IT. Not her. IT.

Wow, she's good at this.

Double whammy.

Well done, Kerstin. Now we've established that I'm the baddie and we have to be worried about how hurt *you* are – not how hurt I was/am, or how let down I feel . . . I get it! A hierarchy of hurts. Plus you still didn't bother to find out anything about the news report for me.

Despite all your promises.

Double double whammy.

I take a deep breath. I reassure myself: *In my last message I was simply stating my feelings.* Detach.

Don't get defensive.

Observe. Don't absorb.

I adjust my visor. I grip my breathing tube in between my teeth. I'll be OK. The bullets marked *You know that is utterly untrue* don't hurt at all. She can't see inside my brain and know what I know. My beliefs are safe.

Christ, how I wish I could go to Fletcher right now and stop playing this stupid death match.

I must not resort to old tactics; I will not offer Kerstin a biscuit.

I hope she gets fat.

I hate myself for thinking that.

I will try to be honest and open and willing . . . I probably *was* blaming her.

I don't want to play games.

I don't want to hate myself.

I actually was blaming her.

She has a point. My email was toxic.

I don't want to hate her.

I was upset.

Kerstin draws in another breath.

I brace myself.

'To be honest,' she says, 'I take the view that we have to be extremely cautious not to be seen to be meddling in business that we have no right to meddle in.'

Surely my past *is* my business?

'There are evil people out there who, in covering their own arses, are ready to point fingers and take us down.'

WHAAA?

Where did that come from?

WHO? WHY?

Uh?

That's crazy, paranoid thinking!

Kerstin adjusts her skirt very deliberately. 'And we have to be aware of their agenda.'

That use of the word 'we'! Such an insidious attempt to plant *her* ideas inside *my* head.

'It's actually very dangerous to poke about and stir things up, especially given the spotlight on police practices and child abuse cases at the moment.'

Crikey. We're in some kind of conspiracy theory!

And she's the sane one.

I blink.

Rapidly.

Let me get this right: she can't help me in case her inquiries about my past are seen as part of a dangerous, countrywide, political witch-hunt against the police by anti-child-abuse campaigners?

Wow! Ten out of ten for the most original excuse of the year!

Checkmate.

I surrender.

'Reality isn't always fair – you can't expect it to be,' she carries on. 'Friends should be able to investigate freely for you but it's not always possible.'

Watch out! Dodge!

The 'we' word is small but deadly.

'I've given this a lot of thought and we don't live in a free world so we have to play the game sensibly. There are loads of other things, as your friend, I can do to support you. You know I've always supported you. Think of all those aphorisms.'

Reproachful silence.

I'm lost. I can't get my head around this.

Kerstin glances down at a notepad, concealed inside her massive designer shoulder bag.

'And to show you that I don't hold any grudges, I've created some more aphorisms for you. And a new list of all your fabulous qualities.'

I give up. I let the rubber suit bounce everything off me. At the end of the day, she wasn't prepared to do a little sleuthing for me, so everything she says is merely her squirming, trying to shed the blame.

God bless diving suits.

She rips a page out and slaps it down in front of me. 'Darling, you have to think twice before you lash out at people.'

Oh no. It's not over.

Here it comes: the atom bomb. Having succeeded at rationalizing her lack of support, she's *now* going to annihilate me.

Classic defensive Cluster B, manipulative thinking. Thank God for Judith's Cognitive Behavioural Therapy otherwise I'd never have noticed it in time.

I give up. I pick up the plate of biscuits and treats and offer her one. Five goodies with a minimum of 130 calories each. And I'm immensely pleased when she chooses the cream-topped, triple-chocolate 488 total calorie muffin.

I'm now officially at the bottom of the ocean.

'I'm not asking for you to hide your feelings from me. We want honesty and openness; we need vibrant, genuine conversation *and* communication. But you need to think about how easy it is to create a misunderstanding.'

Love that pronoun shift.

From 'I' to 'we'.

Then on to 'you'.

Shift the pronoun. Shift the blame

And Heaven spare me from that unrelenting royal WE.'

Why not speak for the whole goddamn world while you're at it, Kerstin?

Speak for everybody.

HELLO. I'm Kerstin. I'm The Voice Of The Universe. LISTEN UP.

'Given the fragile nature of your relationships in general – I mean, you being in here – and that I'm probably the last friend you've got . . .'

Oooh, a shower of napalm. *The last friend I've got!*

'I know you didn't mean to upset me, but I *was* upset and my friendship with you could have been harmed.'

Wow. She knew I didn't mean to upset her. Thanks. She really *is* clairvoyant! That's awesome.

And lest the missiles haven't spattered me enough, or I forget how grateful I should be for forgiving friends like her who visit me in an 'institution', she adds, 'I'm not very comfortable being so direct and honest with you, darling. And I'm sorry if our little chat is distressing. I'm just saying these things because I feel I need to and because I love you. And I'm visiting you because I love you, and I know you're ill. Saying these things isn't easy – I had to have a ciggie before I came, when I was trying to give up, just in order to have the courage. To be really honest with you, I just hate confrontations. You might take this very badly and refuse to see me ever again, but I'm totally doing this in your own best interests. I hope you know that – and that I love you.'

I hate the love card.

I hate the honey-coloured bullets most of all, especially when they are laced with toxic subtext.

I'm finding it very hard to observe and not absorb.

My rubber suit has grown thin. I'm breathless. I must come up from the bottom of the ocean and find real air. I wonder if I've visited with her long enough for my therapists to believe I'm making progress.

I need to find Fletcher.

I need to wash Kerstin off me.

But the bullets just keep coming.

'I've always been there for you in so many ways, freely giving up my spare time to help you, and it's not nice to be told that I'm a rubbish friend. I think you need to pause sometimes and realize the damage you do to those who love you when you say such truly ungrateful and horrible things.' There are tears in her eyes.

I look out of the window.

Oh, Fletch. I'm so sorry. I really did say horrible things to you.

Is this what I have to get used to? Out there? The darkness is seeping in through my diving suit. I'm not sure I can ever get back out into the light.

At the very bottom of the garden, the bushes rustle, leaves are teased apart and from deep inside the greenery the Alien winks at me.

His wink says: Go on, try the Real World. See if it's better than what *we* have. See if you can handle it alone without your little monster.

Kerstin jolts me back into the conservatory, her aggression barely skimmed over with pleasantries.

'Don't you dare attack me again and suggest I don't care about your recovery!' She's getting very shrill. 'Take the hint, Dani. I have my reasons for not doing your research. And don't ever try to guilt me by saying "What goes around comes around."'

Whoa.

She snaps her holdall to. Gives me a quick plastic smile. 'That's all, darling. I've said enough. It's up to you now how you take it, but I strongly urge you to think hard.'

Thank God she's making ending-type remarks. Thank God she's going to go.

I smile brightly.

'Thanks,' I say. 'Sorry.'

Behind the heavy rubber mouthpiece, I stick my tongue out at her.

Then I wonder if she really is clairvoyant and can see through my diving mask.

STEP NINE
INJURE THEM

49

Where is Fletcher?

Kerstin's visit was far too long. It's morning Circle Time now. There is no way I can climb five flights of stairs to go looking. I text him for the third time.

Where the frick are you? I've said I'm sorry. I need to see you. Get here. CT is about to start.

Around me the others try not to fidget. We wait for Tony to get going.

My heart is pounding.

Fletcher has to come.

His chair is empty.

I swear I'll never see Kerstin again.

This is madness.

Despite Tony and all the others, I openly text Fletcher.

GET HERE. I'M SORRY. I HAVE NEWS. IT'S ALL GOING TO BE OK.

'Today we're going to talk about addiction and the lost self.' Tony frowns slightly at me. 'We have a guest speaker in today, especially to talk us through this topic. Her name is Miriam Jaeger and we welcome her to our circle.'

I look across at the strange new woman. I try to overcome my instant dislike of her. She's sitting in the chair that Carmen used to sit in.

'Hi, my name is Miriam. I am an addict,' she says.

'Hi, Miriam,' we respond.

I look at the door. I strain my ears. *He must come.* I try to see if I can hear him. *Fletcher?*

'Tony has kindly invited me here so that I can share with you my model of thinking about recovery.'

'Thank you, Miriam,' we all chorus.

'We're going to be talking about how, as addicts, we cannot act from our innate selves, but organize our thinking around another person, a substance or a process. About how we are, in fact, never really filled up. My feeling is that this emptiness is the result of clinical codependency and it underlies all addiction.'

Where is he?

'Essentially codependency is a mental-health condition. I'm sure you're all aware of its medical definitions and won't confuse it with just being dependent on another or inter-dependent with another. Neither should the term be confused with enabling another, nor even with two people dealing with their needs by relying on and interacting perhaps unhealthily with one another.'

'Yeah, course not,' says Lee, grinning at everyone.

'We must face our codependent selves, developed as a response to our childhood traumas, before we can deal with our addictions,' continues Miriam.

I slide my hand into my pocket, pull out my mobile – just a fraction so nobody can see – and find his number and press 'call'.

'I'm going to give you a visual model to help you under-stand what it is that we as addicts must face. Try to think of an onion. At the core of the onion is the real self. Due to poor or abusive child-rearing practices, this real self is encased by layers of shame-based thinking, a critical inner voice which tells us that we're failures – that we're not good enough, not worthy enough, don't try hard enough. With every year we add more layers of self-hating talk.'

I glance down at my phone.

It's stopped dialling. It offers me a choice of 'call back' or 'voicemail'. I slip it back into my pocket.

'This critical self, covered by onion layers, hides its shame behind a mask. The mask is the projection of the self that we present to the outer world: the self that laughs and smiles, hiding our real selves who aren't smiling, who definitely aren't laughing and who are far too scared to show their true colours.'

Where is he?

'On the very surface of the onion is the perfect self. The perfect self is the self that we would like to be, that self we feel we should have been and that we most definitely are not.'

I try to think of the onion.

I want to speak to Fletcher.

I hate onions. It's always onions, isn't it? It's a good job I've never wanted to eat onion rings. If I had wanted to eat them, my critical self would not have allowed me to. I'm going to hate onions for ever. I allow my perfect self to smile at that.

Fletcher has really blown it now. This is the third time he's missed Circle Time.

Miriam continues, 'Clinical codependency is therefore at the heart of all addiction. And if it goes untreated, like any disease, it will leave the self an empty shell which is then vulnerable to being filled up by addictive processes. Think of it like a room inside you. An empty room. Filled with darkness.'

An empty room.

The Alien is nodding at me, mouthing out, 'BLACK HOLE.'

Fletch? I need you.

'There will be symptoms of denial – denial of the addiction, denial of feelings of shame – and other painful emotions like fear, anxiety, resentment, envy and vengefulness. And of course there will be poor boundaries and that will lead to an overwhelming desire to control. I'll say that again: control. Because control is the only tool that the codependent has to try to reorder the world outside themselves so that they don't have to face their own shame.'

The Alien mouths, 'SUCKS YOU IN.'

Miriam smiles at us around the circle.

I mouth back, 'SUCKS TO YOU.'

Obviously nobody has told her about crosstalk. Or perhaps crosstalk doesn't exist when you have finally become your perfect self.

The Alien pulls a sad face.

Miriam pauses as her smile spotlights us one by one. I'm beginning to feel her talk is rather scripted. She has obviously gone round to a lot of addiction recovery centres and shone the same beaming smile on many other recovering addicts.

I try not to dislike her any more than I do already. Maybe it's all because she's sat in Carmen's chair. My less-than-perfect self jumps up and down and says, *You're in denial – that's why you don't like her.*

My inner critic shouts: *You are a codependent anorexic addict. Fletcher hates you. Kerstin hates you.*

'In short, you codependents are always seeking to change the world rather than yourselves,' she continues, 'because your happiness and your feelings about yourself are located outside yourself.'

I'm beginning to get rather tired of all this You, You, You Stuff.

'Your inner script may run something like this: I've got to make sure that everybody likes me. I must never say "no" and I must please everyone all the time. I've got to be the prettiest/ most interesting/kindest/coolest person in the room/on the street/in the universe. That is codependency.'

I think I could be seriously irritated with Miriam Jaeger.

If I had the energy.

She beams round at us again. An empty beam, devoid of feeling.

A cold snake slithers down my spine.

'The real problem comes when you think you know what other people think – and you think you can control it. So you choose fashions, lose weight, have the latest phone in an attempt to control what others think of you, because you imagine you know what they think of such things.'

Sarah Mussi

Miriam stands up and nods at each of us in clockwise order. 'You practise impression management. You search for approval. You fear abandonment. You have low self-esteem. No self-love. And porous ego boundaries.'

Miriam sits down.

The snake farts and a foul smell fills the room.

Miriam does more crosstalk. She smiles around the circle.

We all wait.

I realize the snake is actually the Alien in disguise.

We still wait.

Politely.

Is that it? Just an exercise in defining how crap we are? What about the recovery bit? Isn't she going to tell us how we can access the real self, break through, smash into smithereens all the fakery we've built up and become our perfect selves – like she has?

I don't get it and I don't want to. I want to go and find Fletcher. His seat stares reproachfully back at me.

Fletcher, you idiot. Why aren't you here?

But now she's pointed out how crap we all are, my critical inner-self voice starts on at me with a vengeance.

It's all your fault he's not here.

You're selfish.

If you hadn't been so unkind, he would be here.

You're mean.

Kerstin was right.

You're manipulative.

You're nasty. Of course you are.

You wanted to feast on his pain.

230

You wanted to see him crumble.

You hauled yourself up the stairs to give yourself an ego boost.

You wanted to break him.

You're a monster.

You're a bigger monster than the Alien you carry around.

I can't stop the voice, and it won't let me off the hook, and I know everything that is going to happen will be my fault – my responsibility – and it will all be terrible.

'JUST GOT TO SUCK IT UP THEN,' smirks the Alien.

50

Immediately I think of strategies.

If I could get even up to three points I might have a chance of silencing the voice. Lunch hasn't happened yet and there's still teatime and supper. If I could get three points, I could feel better about myself.

The Alien starts giggling. He mouths out, 'That's all you really care about, isn't it? Feeling fabulous? You don't care at all about what's happening to poor Fletcher.'

I can't stand it any more.

I get up.

I run out of the room.

We're not supposed to do that – sometimes if you leave Circle Time before you've been dismissed it counts as a strike.

But I don't care.

I've got to find Fletcher.

I don't want to do strategies any more.

I must make him see I'm genuinely sorry.

I must find him and force him to come back to Circle Time – before it ends.

We can face it together. We can still be OK.

Stupid Miriam. I hate Carmen. I hate the world. My heart is pounding like I'm running a marathon. My legs are so weak. I race through the front lobby. I don't care if Judith comes out of her office looking astonished. I glance at her door as I take a corner in the hall. It's slightly ajar. She's interviewing a new client. It won't look good if one of us is having a meltdown.

I don't care.

I need to find Fletcher.

This isn't about Judith.

The newcomer will have to take their chances. I don't even know if they'll sign up to the programme anyway.

I've got to shut my inner critic up. It's beating on me so hard. Just think about Fletcher.

Through the corridors and the stairwells, I hear Carmen shrieking with laughter.

I hear Tony's voice. Poor Tony. He was the only one who tried to stop Fletcher.

He was the only one who tried to be real.

If I run up five full flights of stairs that will be suicide.

I know it's dangerous.

I know it's breaking the rules.

I'll get kicked out.

The lift is strictly out of bounds.

I take the lift.

I make it to Fletcher's room. I knock on the door. The door creaks open. I burst in. I look around.

There's no one there. No stuff. Even Fletcher's smelly pile of shoes in the corner has gone. The windows are wide open. I can't get my brain around it.

What's happened?

Have I gone into the wrong room by mistake?

One of the house staff comes in. She's carrying a pile of folded laundry.

'Where's Fletcher?' I say. 'What have you done with him?'

'Fletcher?' she says, surprised.

'Yes! Fletcher!'

'You mean the boy who was in this room?'

'Yes, the boy who was in this room!' I'm shouting. It's not her fault. Why is she being so stupid?

'You don't know?' she says.

Obviously not.

'He left,' she says.

'*Left?*'

'He's no longer on the programme,' she says.

'What?'

'It's not my business to talk about the clients.'

'*Please?*'

'The boy who was in this room checked out of the programme late last night,' she says. 'He's not coming back.'

I can't take that in.

I don't know what to do. I can't believe he's not here.

The woman stops stripping down the bed. She looks at me like she just wants to get on with the job. But I can't leave. It's like roots have grown out of my feet and attached themselves through the carpet to the floorboards beneath.

'Where's he gone?' I whisper.

She shrugs. 'You need to ask Mr Tony,' she says.

The roots on my feet wither. I leave the room. Behind me, in a whirlwind, is the Alien. I know he's following. I don't turn round and look at him.

Out on the landing, I slam my back against the wall. I push it with the palms of my hands. Then I take out my mobile. We're not supposed to use our mobiles openly in public places. We're not supposed to use our mobiles at all.

It goes to voicemail.

I punch in Fletcher's number again.

It goes to voicemail.

It goes to voicemail.

It goes to voicemail.

It goes to voicemail.

It goes to voicemail.

It goes to voicemail.

'It's me. I'm sorry. You didn't have to go. It's not too late. Please come back. I'm sorry. I'm sorry. I'm sorry. I've got things to tell you. I'm sorry.'

I walk down the stairs.

I try his number seven more times. Seven more times it goes to voicemail.

I stand in the hall outside Tony's office.

Tony's in there. I can hear him talking to somebody.

My knees are shaking.

I try again. *He has to answer. He's not there. Voicemail. He's not there. He's not there.*

I knock on the door.

The conversation inside suddenly goes quiet.

I wait.

I hear a chair being shoved back.

I wait.

The door opens.

Judith walks out.

She gives me one of those looks. It says: We have boundaries for a reason. Boundaries keep us safe. Her look says: You are an addict; you have no boundaries. You were born without them. You grew without them. You don't know who you are – what is you, what is not you. I am very sorry for you. You are out of touch with your feelings. You flood out everywhere. You drown people. You are a nightmare. I thank God I am not you.

I barge into Tony's office.

Tony's office is very male. Black leather armchair. Smooth, polished black desk. Dark laminate flooring. Empty white walls. Concealed glossy black shelves. Chrome filing cases. No pictures.

'Where is he?' I say.

'Sit down,' he says.

I stand.

'Where is he?' I repeat.

'Dani, you can't walk into this office and demand answers. There are protocols. We have to follow them.'

I laugh. I laugh in his pockmarked, middle-aged, prison-challenged face. Is this the same person who was up in Fletcher's room only yesterday, bawling him out?

Then I get it. We must all put on our fake faces. I wonder

if Tony wears a bulletproof suit like mine. I haven't got my suit on now. Hundreds of bullets are going right through me.

'I want to know where Fletcher is.'

Perhaps there's something in the tone and pitch – in my shrieking. Perhaps Tony recognizes something of himself. Some shade of last night, some shadow of the person he might have been if whatever happened to him had not happened.

His voice gentles. 'At least sit down.'

I sit. I put myself on the edge of the visitor's couch.

'Please,' I say.

He sighs.

I can see he's suffering too.

'Fletcher has misused his chances. He was asked to choose between deciding to embrace his future somewhere else, or waiting for the centre to ask him to leave. He chose to go. He was asked not to make any contact with other clients. He's gone.'

'I don't want the official line,' I say.

'You know very well what's happened.'

I perch on the edge of the sofa. I don't know where to start, whether to nod my head or not. I have no idea what's happened. I HAVE ABSOLUTELY NO KNOWLEDGE OF WHAT HAS HAPPENED. I cannot accept anything that has happened.

'Here we try to learn to embrace the now. There's no point in fighting what is,' Tony says.

I just look up at him and wait.

'Fletcher made his choices,' he continues.

I still wait.

'Fletcher misused his chances,' Tony repeats.

So that's it? We only get so many chances in this life, and when we misuse them we're returned to the crap heap? But Fletcher obviously left before he'd missed three meetings anyway. Tony is spouting rubbish. I open my mouth to tell him.

Tony pre-empts me. 'I know,' he says. 'I know Fletcher didn't stay on to exhaust his chances. And for that, Dani, I think I respect him.'

Respect him? You should have stopped him. You didn't try hard enough. It must be somebody's fault. I'm going to blame YOU, Tony.

I don't want to blame myself. It's all my fault though. I sit struggling with whose fault it is.

'He did the right thing,' Tony says.

How can leaving your recovery programme unfinished, staying unrecovered for ever, be the right thing? How can going back to where he came from, to all the pressures and the pain, be the goddamn, effing RIGHT THING?

'Recovery is not easy, and Fletcher recognized he wasn't ready to do the work.'

How can facing all that alone, without me, EVER be the right thing?

'The right thing for the centre too. Fletcher recognized that he wasn't ready to use his place here properly.'

Tony turns his gaze to the window. Broken eyes. A life gone stale.

'We can't change people or control them,' Tony says sadly. 'Fletcher has to make his own choices.'

238

Oh, spare me!

'I think you need to do a little bit of stocktaking too,' Tony says.

Stocktaking? Excellent! So now it's my fault. I'm a Director Of The Universe and everything that happens is my responsibility!

I'm in control of the world.

Blame me if everything goes wrong.

'There are many roads to Rome,' Tony says uneasily.

I notice that I may have picked bald a patch of pile on the sofa. I try to hide the fluff in a little ball. I cover the bald patch with my hand.

'Take heart,' says Tony. 'Even if Fletcher didn't show the commitment needed to his recovery this time round, it's not the end of the story.' He smiles at me through gold-capped, half-missing front teeth.

But in the dead centre of his eyes, I can see he's a zombie. He has drunk the blood of the goddess Kali. Last night when he pushed past me on the landing, his eyes were alive. He was awake and on fire. The real person was there. Now he's completely undead.

And lying.

In this programme they don't allow failures. Everybody is a success. If you look like you're not going to make it, they'll force you out. They must be so pissed off about Carmen. Why can't Tony just say it?

'Where's he gone?' I ask.

'I'm afraid I can't give you that information, Dani.'

'Why not?'

'You know exactly why not.'

239

'He'd want me to have it.' I know he would.

'When a client leaves this programme,' Tony says, 'we make them aware that they must not contact anyone still within the programme. It isn't healthy. It would negatively impact the recovery of others.'

I look at him. There are some things I just don't get about this real world.

'We can't pass on any confidential information, even if we wanted to,' he says in that kind way adults have of trying to tell some juvenile the unacceptable. 'It's not allowed under the Data Protection Act.'

Enough.

Hiding behind the Data Protection Act.

I stand up. I face Tony.

'You're a fraud,' I yell. 'You're a fake, phoney, empty con man. You were probably more real when you were in prison. You should've stayed there. Look at you.'

I just scream, 'LOOK AT YOURSELF! LOOK AT YOURSELF! LOOK AT YOURSELF!'

I turn round to leave.

I'd like to run, but I can't.

I slam the door instead.

51

I slam my bedroom door behind me too.

Thank God I don't have a goddamn roommate. I sit down on my bed. I smack my head down on the pillow. He's gone. He's left me. He doesn't care. Nobody ever cares. It's because I'm ugly. Because I'm fat. Because I'm the wrong shape. My legs are too short; my ankles are too thick. I'm a mess. I'm a monster. I drove him away. It's my fault. I always drive everyone away. I never do the nice thing, the caring thing. I'm a monster.

I'm an Alien.

My hair is too thin. My eyes are too small. Face too fat. I hate my cheeks – my great, round, podgy, soggy, pudding cheeks. And I'm going bald.

Something looks in at the window. *Tap tap.*

I look up. A little head is poking itself over the sill. It smiles wistfully at me. It's a smile that says: I'm still here, you know. I'm still your friend. Just let me in again.

I sit up on the bed. I think I'm going to open the window and invite the Alien back in.

But as I move across the room, I look out through the window, across the garden, past the honeysuckle wall, out into Berkshire. I remember those eyes, Fletcher's eyes, that day when we made our first pact – about being real, about promising to be buddies.

What happened?

How did it all fall apart?

The Alien gives me a winning smile. It looks like a little kitten with a little white spot on its nose. Little pink tongue and big, big, blue-brown eyes.

But I sit back down on the bed. I swallow a piece of steel. I made a promise to Fletcher. I promised I would be there for him. And I haven't been.

So I give up?

Is that the deal?

Conditional love?

Limited liability?

I don't want that kind of love any more. Because I was loved. And I realize it's true. Fletcher loved me and my mother loved me.

My mother loved and loved and loved me.

Unconditionally.

When your mother loved you and died for you, conditional love is not enough any more.

I've grown out of being the kind of person who tries to do a little bit less and get a little bit more.

I want to be unlimited.

My mother starved to death for me. She gave me food when there was none.

So I sadly shake my head at the Alien. It sticks out its pink tongue, which becomes black and poisonous and huge.

My fingers flutter. A shaking starts inside. There's a quivering going on in my stomach. A tsunami starts somewhere in the mid-Atlantic and builds.

I know that I'm breaking one of the innermost rules of my being.

I MUST ALWAYS DO WHAT THE ALIEN WANTS.

But I'm not going to.

I'm not going to be someone who goes back on a deal. Fletcher was my recovery buddy. Whether he's here or not, I have a responsibility to recover because my mother died for me. Because I was loved.

I sit up. I pick up my hand mirror.

I'm going to try a recovery exercise.

I look at my face in the mirror and, standing over my shoulder, I imagine the person I love most in all the world.

I gaze into the mirror. I don't even know who I love most. I try very hard to see the face of my mother. But I cannot. My eyes fill with tears. I can't remember her. The tsunami grows seven metres tall. I feel like I'm going to vomit.

If I went back into the room, would I find her face?

Would I remember her?

Judith showed me the way. Go back to your earliest memory. Open the door beyond it. My heart pounds.

I must find my mother.

Her face lies behind that door.

In the empty room.

I go back to my earliest memory. I go back to the closed

door. I start to hyperventilate. I put my hand on the door-knob. I twist. I push. I can't open the door.

It's locked against me.

I stand up. I do three little jumping jacks.

I'm not going to do jumping jacks any more. They belong to the poor, disordered, old me.

I sit down on the bed again. I pick up the mirror a second time.

I look into the space over my shoulder to see the face of the person I love most. In the gloom behind me, somewhere on the blue wallpaper, is the face of Fletcher.

I'm surprised. Is that who I love most?

Unconditionally and for ever?

And the tsunami hits.

A flood washes over me.

I love Fletcher?

I didn't even know.

I didn't know this feeling was called love.

I love Fletcher.

I love him in a totally unlimited way.

And I must recover.

I say to Fletcher's face, 'You're ugly. You're fat. You're misshapen. Your hair is too thin. You're going bald. Your ankles are too thick. Nobody can love you. Look at you. You can't stand up straight. You're too short. Your fingers are too stubby.' I tell him everything that I've been telling myself.

I feel voodoo pins sticking into my hands and arms and shoulders with every insult, until I can't say them any more. I can't tell him he's ugly. I can't tell him he's misshapen. I can't tell him anything so hurtful. And if I can't tell the person I love most in all the world these terrible things then why should I tell them to myself?

Now I try to say, 'You're pretty. You're normal. You're lovable.' I can't get the words out. In my mind I go over and over the words: 'You're lovable, you're pretty, you're right just the way you are.'

I break out into a cold sweat.

The Alien raps and raps on the glass.

The water level is nearly window high. Outside, trees and cars race past in the flood.

'Let me in,' wails the Alien.

I think of Fletcher out there on the streets.

I must do this.

'You are fine just the way you are,' I say to my reflection in the mirror.

It comes out in a whisper.

The Alien shatters into a thousand little fragments of bone and clatters down on to the windowsill and is swept away.

And I know what I must do, whether or not Fletcher is here.

STEP TEN
WHEN WE WERE WRONG

52

Slowly I go down the stairs to the refectory. It's lunchtime. I pick up a tray from the counter. I join the queue. It's a brown tray with a smooth wood-like feel to it. It's moulded into a normal rectangular shape. I love normal.

I pick up my cutlery: knife and fork and spoon. They're normal spoons and normal forks and normal knives. I slide my tray along the very normal chrome rails of the buffet counter. And I think about what I'm going to eat.

There's a basket full of little rolls – some are white, some brown; some have seeds on them. I haven't tasted bread in over eight years. I pick up a normal white roll, soft with a slightly creamy golden crust over its top. I put it down on my side plate. I see the butter, little tiny squares in silver and gold foil. I think about the creamy taste of butter. I'm not sure I can allow myself butter, but there's a wildness inside me, an abandonment, as if nothing really matters any more or every-thing matters all the more, and it's thrumming through me . . . so I pick up one of the little squares of normal butter!

I feel the slight squidginess of the tiny packet. I put it beside the roll. Am I mad?

I slide my tray further on along the counter.

The menu today is chicken and mushroom casserole with mashed potato and peas. The vegetarian option is cheese and courgette lasagne. And here's the salad bar at the end. I long to try the creamy, cheesy lasagne. My mouth begins to salivate in a distressing way. My throat gulps.

I get to the vegetarian section. The woman behind the counter looks at me. She's surprised when I lift up my tray. She turns and nudges one of the other servers behind the counter. The woman stops serving a great slop of mushroom and chicken on to the next girl's plate and looks at me.

I try not to look back. I try to stop the negative talk which is telling me: *They think I'm ugly; they think I'm bulimic; they think I'll get fat; they think I shouldn't be eating. They think I've been pretending. They think I'm a fraud.*

I stop myself.

It's just a plate of lasagne.

It's very normal to eat at lunchtime.

I hand over the plate. The food is dished out. I put it on my tray.

'Thank you,' I say.

I slide the tray down to the serve-yourself salad counter.

I've always longed to serve myself and stuff my plate totally full. I'm going to do it.

I spoon on grated carrot. I pile it in a bowl. I move along a bit and scoop up a serving of chopped cucumber and tomato and little pieces of Greek feta cheese.

I'm trembling at the enormity of what I'm doing.

I stop and brace myself against the chrome rails.

Two vegetarian kebabs.

Two!

The tray feels so heavy.

I glance at it. I've become so adept at counting calories, I can see immediately that this whole plate is at least 750, probably more.

Probably more!

I try to shut off the calculator in my head. I'm working out the ratio of jumping jacks to calories, how many hours I'd have to walk up and down the garden to burn off that lot.

With trembling hands I move towards the far table by the window, the table where I used to sit and eat nothing and watch the others chewing.

And I don't know what to eat first. And it all looks so much. How can I possibly eat everything on my plate?

But I'm going to try.

I'm going to try to get well now.

My mother wants me to eat.

Fletcher needs me, and if I can get well, if I can keep my end of the bargain, then I can leave here. I will find him. I will help him. I will.

So I pull a bit of bread off the side of the bun. I open the foil wrapper on the butter. I shave a sliver of butter away from the little pat and spread it over the bread.

And I find that I can easily open my mouth and put it inside!

Oh, the taste of the butter!

It spreads like a sunset inside my mouth, over my tongue in a golden glow. The bread has a soft, rich, gooey flavour, and I'm totally amazed at the awesomeness of it.

I pick up the fork. I ladle up some cheese sauce with a slice of courgette snuggled into it. I balance it on the prongs of the fork and my mouth is open again, ready.

I've never been able to open my mouth like this before. Everybody must be watching. The universe must see: I can open my mouth!

And now I'm eating cheesy courgette with pasta. My mouth is exploding, like all the fireworks in the universe have been let off inside my taste buds. Suddenly it's not hard to swallow. This must surely be a miracle.

And I'm doing this for me, because I was loved. I'm doing this because I keep my word. Because I'm keeping my deal with my lovely, awesome, kind recovery buddy. Because I know that somewhere out there on the streets, Fletcher hopes that I will.

Because I believe in a world that believes in me.

Because I am normal.

And the whole world won't starve because I'm eating. I look up from the cheesy pasta, and everyone is eating. Tears well up in my eyes and roll down my face and plop into the grated carrot and I don't mind. I'm going to eat my tears, eat my sadness and then it will all be gone for ever.

And as I lift the fork again to taste some of the coleslaw, a voice beside me says, 'Can I join you?'

I look up, and it's the girl who has replaced Carmen. She looks very thin. I know that look. There's nothing on her tray apart from a glass of water and some lettuce. She drags at the chair opposite me and sits down.

I'm tempted to say, 'What strategy are you playing? Do you think that by watching me eat you'll be happy? Do you think that my every mouthful makes you better or more lovable?'

And I want to tell her that it doesn't. That the only thing that can help her to recover is finding out why she doesn't want to.

The only thing that will make her happy is knowing, deep inside, that she's worth it.

I know she'd like to eat everything on my plate. I know she's fainting inside with the longing of it.

But today is my day and I'm going to eat it. I'm going to eat my lunch, everything on my plate, and I'm not going to binge it out afterwards.

I smile at her.

'I'm looking for my recovery buddy,' she says.

I nod. It's one of the hardest parts when you're new in the programme, the whole recovery buddy thing.

'Who have they assigned you to?' I ask.

She doesn't answer. She pushes the salad leaf around her plate.

And suddenly I understand.

Fletcher has been erased.

Fletcher does not exist any more.

Fletcher is gone.

I am her recovery buddy.

53

I finish my meal. I have to. That's the deal. I feel bloated and huge and it hurts. But I do it.

Then I have to get out of the refectory.

Fletcher is my recovery buddy.

Not her.

I want to support this new girl, but she can't be my recovery buddy. Not yet anyway. It's like being on a plane during an emergency – I have to put my oxygen mask on first.

Then on Fletcher.

NOBODY CAN EVER, EVER, EVER REPLACE FLETCHER.

Because I love him.

Unconditionally.

Unlimited liability.

And I'm feeling its sting for the first time.

But can love be exclusive? Unconditional love is for every-one, isn't it? It's such a strange concept. I look at the girl, Alice

251

Munro. Do I love her at all? It's too weird. I wish I could do for her what Fletcher tried to do for me. But I can't.

I need saving.

He needs saving.

But so does she.

That's a true dilemma.

But Fletcher is my first and best recovery buddy. I'm not healed enough to help Alice yet. I'm not healed enough to help anyone apart from Fletcher.

I need oxygen. I need to think. I need fresh air. I tried so hard. I need to breathe.

I leave Alice. I step out of the back door of the centre. I walk across the short terrace. Down two steps to our honeysuckle, compost corner. I can still taste the thick, cheesy clinginess of the lasagne. Suddenly I feel sick. I feel like vomiting.

I can't do this.

It's too much.

I turn to go back to the centre. I stop myself. Solve the dilemma. I take a deep breath. Stay with yourself. Unconditional love is just that. Unconditional. Stay by the honeysuckle. Fletcher would tell you to. Stay in the dilemma. One day at a time. You must recover. You must complete the programme. You will not betray your mother's love.

You will not let her down.

Or Fletcher.

You need to get stronger.

Or yourself.

I pause. The sick giddy feeling passes. I won't go back inside. I will recover.

I stand there as frail as a piece of tissue blowing in the wind. I clutch hold of the wall. I will stay here. I will stay true.

And like the answer to a prayer, my phone rings.

The name flashes up.

Fletch.

'Hello,' I whisper.

I can't believe it. It's a reward. It's a reprieve. It's like a shooting star in the cosmos.

'I'm sorry,' I whisper. 'I didn't mean those things.'

'That's OK,' he says.

I don't say, 'But I'm glad we quarrelled. I mean, I'm not glad, but because we quarrelled I understood. I've remembered everything.'

But I want to say that.

'I'm on the streets.' He laughs.

'Why, Fletcher?' I say.

'I'm not going back over that again,' he says.

Of course he's not going over it again. He's on the streets.

I have no idea what it's like being on the streets.

'Where?'

'It's just a street, like any other street – and I'm just thinking about using all the time. I need to find money.'

'Can't we try again?'

Laughter. 'Yeah, course, find me a new recovery centre?'

'What happens now?' I ask.

'Have you got any money you could lend me?' he says.

I have nothing, absolutely nothing.

Wrong.

I have got some money. I could lend it to him. But not if it's just going to go up his nose.

'I'm hungry,' he says. 'I haven't eaten since I left the centre.'

I laugh and I don't laugh. At least I have eaten.

'Will you come and talk to me?' I ask. 'I have things to say.'

'I'm not allowed to visit and you know that,' he says.

'We could meet at the bottom of the garden,' I say. 'I'm standing here right now.'

'Meet and do what?' he says.

'Talk,' I say.

'So *now* you want to talk! When it's far too late to say anything worth saying.' He laughs.

I want to shout out: BUT I UNDERSTAND NOW. I WANT TO RECOVER. I want to tell you.

I stop myself. I swallow the words. I don't want to reel him back into saving me. I want to be there for him.

'Look, can you meet me or not?'

'If they find us talking then you'll be chucked out too,' says Fletcher. 'Are you really willing to risk that?'

'It's not about them any more,' I say. 'It's not about their rules. You're my recovery buddy and I need to tell you things.'

I don't know any other way of reaching out to him.

'OK,' he says finally.

'You'll meet me then?' I say.

'Where?' he says.

'Here at the bottom of the garden. Meet me tonight after supper, about 8:30, after it gets dark. I'll bring you food. I'll be waiting.'

54

At the bottom of the garden, by the wall where the honey-suckle grows, I wait for Fletcher.

Why is it that in the evening, after rain, everything smells so much more powerful? I'm almost in the locked room.

I'm holding a curtain around me. I think it's a curtain. I don't want to see the body of my mother slumped across the doorway. But the perfume of honeysuckle won't let me be. And I can hear the sounds of planks banging together. The squeal of the iron gates of the timber yard.

If I listen carefully, I can even hear the sound of men's voices talking, the repeated revving of an engine far away. I pull the curtain tighter, but the scent of honeysuckle stays.

'Dani?'

He came.

I don't know what I was thinking. A part of me believed he wouldn't come. Perhaps I hoped too much that he would. I've learned in life that when you want something too much, you must prepare for the pain.

'Dani?' he says again.

A rush and the flood, and I realize just how much I do want him here. How lonely I've been since yesterday morning.

'Fletch?' I whisper.

There's a real, warm, full-bodied rustling overhead, and the noise of breaking and cracking. A hole appears in the honeysuckle as its trailers are stretched and snapped back. Then a dark anorak, a pale face and legs kicking through the undergrowth. Nothing like the Alien. Here beside me, pulling leaves out of his hair, is a real live Fletcher.

For some stupid reason I want to throw my arms around him. I start towards him. I see the same feeling fireworking in him. He takes a step. We both stop. I put my hands behind my back. Then in my pockets.

I forget about the food. I remember about the food. I go back to the bench and pick up the plastic bag with the banana and a bread roll and a leg of chicken in foil. I feel shy. I hold it out. This is weird. I try to remember if I have ever given food to anyone without scoring a point. And I realize this is a very first.

'You said you were hungry,' I say.

Fletcher sits down on the bench, tears open the foil. 'Thanks,' he says, his mouth full.

'I'm sorry,' I say.

'Um,' he says. He nods his head.

'What are we going to do?' I say.

I search his face. It's still the same old him. He's trying to stay clean. Brave Fletcher. He hasn't used yet.

Fletcher swallows, wipes the crumbs from around his mouth with his sleeve and pulls a smile that is a goddamn awful fake smile.

There's still a chance we can recover.

'Take it one goddamn day at a time,' Fletcher says.

'Please,' I say. 'We don't have a lot of time.'

Fletcher sighs. 'I know, but it hurts to be real with you.'

'What are you going to do?' I ask.

I want to tell him about the third person in the room. I want to ask him to help me to find out who it was. I want to return to those days. I want to see my mother's face. Those evenings. When we were detectives. On the case. Together. Discovering about ourselves. Unravelling the most important mystery of all: who we are. When I didn't know how much I needed him. If only he would help me now. He could go to the room – he's free from the rehab now.

I catch myself – free? On the streets? But we could be a team again. We could. It would be all about me, but I wouldn't have to be so alone.

'I don't know,' he says.

I don't say anything.

'Yeah, yeah, yeah,' he says.

I understand. It's not about just stopping using. It's about that empty hole inside. It's about shutting down that voice which says: *You're shit. You're nothing. What will happen? You're a loser. You have nowhere to live. You're hopeless. You'll die. You're broken. Terrible things will happen to you. You can never recover. Never. Never. It will be awful. Everybody hates you. Where are your friends?* And it talks so quickly. And pours such poison into your ear, every waking moment, that it's no good just saying, *Think positive*.

If only.

It won't give you the space to.

I try a different way. 'OK, tell me about the hole.'

For a moment he looks puzzled, then he sighs. 'It started so long ago. I can't even remember how young I was.

'But here is one memory. My earliest. I guess I must have been very young. I think I'd soiled myself. I remember being uncomfortable and crying. I was hungry too. I remember always being hungry. My mum had probably been drinking, although I didn't know about drinking then. All I knew was that she could be in a happy mood, a wild mood, and then she slept and after she woke up she'd be in a black mood.

'Later I realized it was best not to talk to her then. To hide. Stay clear. Shut myself away. That time, I remember her telling me to shut up. I didn't know how to. She got really mad. She said, "If you don't shut up I'm going to put you in a cooking pot and boil you and eat you." That made me cry more. It terrified me. She got down a huge pan, a really old style one – when I see pans like that now, I start trembling. She grabbed me. She pinched me. She sat me on the chopping board. She pushed her face right up against mine and said, "I'm going to boil you. I'm going to eat you." I was screaming and screaming.

' "There's only one way you can save yourself and that is to SHUT UP," she said.'

I can feel Fletcher's terror even now, so many years later.

'She took a jug and filled it at the sink. She poured the water into the cauldron. She got out some salt and pepper and sprinkled it all over me. She even chopped up a carrot and threw it into the water. I can still hear the knife thudding through the carrot right beside me. I sat there covered in salt and pepper, and I learned to shut up.

'After that, when she told me to do anything, I did it straight away. There were other things . . .' His voice trails off.

I understand: the damage was done. I don't have anything to say. I'm not sure that even Judith, with all her psycho-therapeutic training, or Tony, with all his prison years of twelve-step programmes, can undo that kind of damage.

'I didn't have a choice back then,' says Fletcher. 'I didn't have a dad. And if my mum wasn't there, I didn't know what would happen to me.

'She used to tell me that if she got ill and died, they would take me away. She told me they'd take me away and put me in a big hole in the ground. That I'd feel the earth all around me until I couldn't breathe. And then they'd put more earth over my head and stamp the soil flat, and that would be the end of me.

'Sometimes she'd say that she'd give me away to them anyway, even if I did do what she wanted, or that one day I might wake up and she would just be gone. Gone away. Gone off to live her life, without a child to take care of, without any responsibilities. She'd say that I had spoilt it all for her. What was she supposed to do with a baby to look after? How could she get a job? Or go out and have fun?'

I want to ask Fletcher to forgive his mother. But I'm find-ing that hard.

'She made me into her slave. I tried to do everything right. I tried to cheer her up, and raced down to the corner and bought her alcohol, and fixed her tea when she had a headache, and listened to all her stories about how she could've been somebody, how she was born to be great, and how it was all my fault, because if she hadn't had a baby she would've been rich and famous somewhere, somehow.'

'She was sick,' I say. 'Let it go.'

'There wasn't any me left,' says Fletcher. 'I just poured myself into her. I was there because she needed me to be there. I don't think I even remembered who I was most of the time. And I was terrified that she would die or abandon me, and then I would be nothing. I would have nothing. And the hole inside me grew and grew into a deep black bottomless pit. That threatened to suck me in.

'I tried so hard to keep her alive,' he says. 'I begged her to go and find help from someone. But she got so angry if I tried to suggest there was anything wrong with her. Once I saved up some coins and went out and bought a pretty dress for her. I thought it was pretty. I was only about nine, I guess. I bought it from a charity shop. I remember exactly how much it was: ninety-five pence. I bought it because she was always complaining she couldn't go out and have a life, because she had nothing to wear, because all the money went on feeding me. I thought if she went out and found some friends it would help her. She might be happier. I wanted her to be happy. I didn't know anything about dress sizes, but I thought it looked big enough to fit her. But when I gave her the dress she flew into a rage. She accused me of terrible things. She said, "A nasty old dress from a charity shop – what kind of child are you? Do you want your mother to look like a tramp?"

'She said a lot of things. I've forgotten them. I got used to doing that – not hearing stuff. But I felt it. That's strange, isn't it? I felt her anger, like blows inside my chest, yet I don't remember what she said.'

'Why didn't you say any of this at Circle Time?' I ask, but I know why. Who wants to talk about all that in front of Judith?

Fletcher shrugs. 'It would have sounded disloyal. I loved my mum. And if Judith had asked me one more time, "How does that make you feel?", I think I might have punched her.'

I laugh.

'But it feels good to tell you,' he says.

55

'I'm sorry.'

'It wasn't your fault,' he says.

'It was, partly,' I say. 'I should've tried harder.'

'No, it wasn't,' he says. 'I was doing my old stuff, trying to take care of you, and not taking care of myself. I was terrified.'

'I'm sorry,' I say again.

'I was terrified you'd die. And I'd be alone. I was terrified they'd put you in a hole in the ground. I was terrified that you didn't want to be my recovery buddy any more, so I just decided to leave the programme.'

'But how has that helped? I don't get it.'

'The thing about the streets is that they're always there. Once you're homeless you don't have to be afraid of being abandoned and rejected and left out – because you already are. So there's a weird kind of security in that. It just felt too hard to keep on trying. I gave up. It just felt safer.'

'But you threw everything away,' I say. Maybe I still don't get it.

'I threw it away before you threw *me* away,' he says. 'It just made it easier. I don't think I could have borne it if you'd rejected me or died.'

Fletcher has such a long way to go. He's totally making me his Higher Power again, and though it's flattering it's not right.

'And you quarrelled with me,' he says, 'and you told me all about myself. And I knew there wasn't any point in anything any more. So I left.'

'I'm so sorry,' I say.

'I was never mad at you . . . I was mad at myself. I was mad at the world. I'm still mad at the world.'

'That's no good though.' I say. 'Think of everything we've learned. However much we don't like the way we learned it, it's true – some of that stuff is really true. Even Judith says stuff that really does make sense. I mean, we can't control the world even if we stop eating altogether. We can't escape it. We're stuck with reality – big time.'

Fletcher giggles.

'We can't control things and we're not the cause of them,' I say.

'We're pretty much losers from the start.'

'Yeah.'

'Tough.'

'Yeah.' I put on a Judith voice: 'All you can do is choose not to let the past have power over the future.'

Fletcher smiles. 'At last the penny drops. Bit late, but there you go.'

'It's never too late,' I say. Then I pause.

He pauses too.
The moment lingers.
Then I tell him my big news.
The honeysuckle quivers.
The blackbird sends out one last sweet note.
'I ate lunch today,' I say.

56

'You what?' he says.

'And supper,' I say.

Fletcher's face lights up. I can see he is nowhere near cured. He's pouring himself into me like the Niagara Falls. He's totally delighted I'm starting to recover. Like it's his personal triumph. He's forgotten that it's not.

Suddenly I am all important. Reality has shifted its focus from him over to me. And I can see he prefers it.

'Tell me all about it,' he says.

And I can't resist. The taste of that bread still lingers some-where in visceral memories at the back of my throat. Big creamy buttery feelings.

I start to tell him.

He looks so happy.

I don't stop.

I tell him about it – every bite, every crumb, every swallow. And by the time I've finished, he's smiling so widely; we could almost believe we were sitting somewhere else, at a different and better point in our futures, when we've recovered, when we're together, living in that cheap bedsit, in some kind of Happy At Last future bubble.

'Can we try again?' he says. 'If you carry on eating, I promise I'll try hard. I'll go to meetings. I can find out where they're held. I'll find a sponsor. It's not too late. If you'll eat, I can do anything.'

And what should I say now?

Should I tell him that he should be overjoyed at the thought of his own recovery, not because I ate a roll and a plate of pasta? But somehow it doesn't matter how you get there. It's just important that you do.

So I say, 'Yes, let's try again.'

'We need to swear it on something this time,' he says.

'If I tell you something, do you promise you'll still stay on track?'

'There is nothing you can tell me – as long as we're doing this together – that could change anything,' he says.

So I tell him about the third person.

Instantly Fletcher is all Sherlock Holmes.

He sits on the edge of the bench. His lovely, punch-throwing shoulders don't slouch any more. There's a light in his eyes that is awe-inspiring.

'We need a lead,' he says.

My heart flutters, my blood pounds and my cheeks ache from smiling.

'But there may not be any records of a third person,' I say.

Fletcher thinks about that. 'You're right,' he says. 'There probably won't be.' A tree crashes down in some distant rainforest. 'I'll bet he got away with it, didn't he? He locked you and your mum up. He used and abused you. You starved. Your mum died. And he got away with it.'

The forest floor shakes. The smell of honeysuckle is over-powering. I hold my breath.

'And you've been paying for it ever since,' says Fletcher.

He's angry.

'He really messed you up.' Two high spots of colour have appeared on Fletcher's cheeks. He clenches and unclenches his fists. 'To the point where you've almost starved yourself to death. You can't let – *can't* let him – ever get away with it.'

More trees are falling. They're heading for the timber yard.

'We need to find out who he is,' says Fletcher. 'We'll nail the bastard.'

I shake my head.

Fletcher leans forward, stretches out a hand, taps me on the forehead. He says, 'And we need to get him out of there.'

I nod.

'So you need to remember.'

It's déjà vu.

Nothing's changed.

My hands break into a sweat. Fletcher will take over. My throat dries up. I do not want to remember.

'What if we go back to the room?' says Fletcher. 'What if we go there and do one of those Judith hypnotic things? We might find out who he is.'

He glances up at my face.

He understands.

'Or do you want him to get away with it?' he says. More

trees crash. An earthquake opens up a crack, right under the Atlantic. 'He did that to your mum! He did that to you! *Do you really want to let him get away with it?*'

A fresh tsunami forms. A hurricane blows.

'Think about it,' he says. 'We've worked so hard to get to this point. We found out where the room is; we found out what happened to you; we discovered it wasn't your mum's fault. And it's helped. You ate. *You goddamn ate lunch, Dani!* We can do this. I want to do this. I want to do this for you. I want to be there for you, like we promised. OK?'

I can't tell him. He's so much more fragile than me.

'Let me do this,' he says. 'I'll go there. I'll find out everything. Then you can come and we'll catch the bastard and we'll get closure. I'll wait until you're fully strong enough to leave rehab, till you're recovered, until you've graduated from this programme. I can wait. I'd like to wait. I'll be OK if I know what I'm waiting for. I'll have something to wait for. I can do it.'

I shake my head.

'It'll be like old times. It will work. It'll really help me too,' he says.

But it won't help him. Will it?

It will just be another reason for Fletcher not to work on himself. I would just be helping him to have no boundaries, all over again.

And it won't help me. Because I've got to face my own demons.

Like him.

'We will recover,' I say, 'but not like that. I've got to be strong enough on my own. You've got to be strong enough too – and not just strong for me, Fletch. You've got to be strong for yourself. Because you believe in yourself. Because you can stand alone. Even if you are alone and have to be alone for ever.'

There's this stricken, empty look on his face, like a dog that has been locked out.

'I'm not going to die,' I whisper, 'but I have to face this in my own way.'

I leave the unspoken. *Now Fletcher must go back. Back to the streets, without any mission. Back to face his own demons right there, where they live.*

'You won't be alone,' I whisper. 'Not any more. But you have to face things that are yours. Just as I have to.'

'Like we all have to.'

I can't ask him to do that and not do it myself.

So I make a decision.

The hurricane dies off.

The tsunami subsides.

I will face my demons too.

By myself.

I will do this for me.

And I won't give myself time to change my mind.

Tomorrow I will go to the empty room.

Before I go to sleep, my phone vibrates.

Fletcher.

I can't stop thinking about you, Dani. About how we're trying again. It's bad and it's good. It's so good I'm scared and that's bad. I know. I know. I would say that's No Boundaries, and it's black-and-white thinking when reality is actually all shades of grey. OK, don't let me get on to shades of grey, or I will start thinking about you like that.

Another text.

Q: would you be cross if I did?

I'm so tempted to escape into 'True Love's Kiss'.

I turn my phone off.

I must focus on myself.

And tomorrow.

STEP ELEVEN
THE POWER TO CARRY THAT OUT

57

It is tomorrow.

I am here. I left the rehab centre straight after breakfast. I ate two slices of toast and they're still inside me. I sat on the bus and found it soothing.

I hope Daisy Bank will take me back. It's dangerous to eat too much too suddenly. Tony warned me of eating after starvation. But even if they don't take me back, this has to be my next step.

Step Thirteen. The hardest step of all.

Tony told me of deadly potassium levels.

But today I still ate.

Because today I am facing all my demons.

Today I will face the worst one. Where he lives.

In the empty room.

I have a promise to keep.

To Fletcher.

And myself.

And my mother.

Then we can heal.
With truth and love.
Then I will be strong enough for myself.
And for him.
And for all the Alices of this world.

💣 ☠ 🖤

I think I have the right street but it's hard to tell.

It's mid-morning. I sit down on a low wall. I pull out the notepad.

I look at all of Fletcher's entries: timber yards. The addresses of all the timber yards. Houses likely to have bars on windows. Edwardian? Victorian? Lorries. Roads large enough to admit lorries. Smell? The smell of death? Abattoir? Hospital? Wind direction? South-westerly during the months of November to December. Somewhere near the woodyard. Near honeysuckle.

I'll miss Circle Time.

I must find Arches Timber Ltd, Phoenix Wharf, Mordly Hill Street, Lewisham, London, SE4 9QQ.

But I don't really need Fletcher's notes. Now I'm near, there's a part of me that knows these streets. They're etched on me like scars from cuttings so long ago. Their lorries and air currents flow through my veins. The windy corner by the bus stop. I don't want to be here. I can feel her hand in mine. I can tell by the paving slabs, the cracks, the kerb, the way the drain cover doesn't quite fit.

I know this street. I know all these streets.

They're mine.

I walk them hand in hand with my mother. I must have been so small. Maybe the trees have grown, the walls shrunk. Another person inside me knows the way. My feet are making decisions for me.

That's where there used to be a corner shop. A sweet shop. A symphony of sugar. And my mother came here with me, her face brimming with light. Here there were Lovehearts. My mum used to read them to me. A feeling lifts me. I rise skywards, soaring into sunshine.

My mother was here with me.

Reading Lovehearts.

Once in another world.

I feel the memory like a zephyr in my chest. Quivering. Straining. Here on these very paving stones, I remember her putting a pale-lemon-coloured Loveheart on my tongue. It read: *You Are Cute.*

It tasted so sweet.

She told me it was true.

My eyes fill with tears. I want to fall on my knees and lay my cheek on the paving stones.

My mother stood here and she loved me. And I was cute. And we ate Lovehearts.

And on the opposite side of the road, there was a duck pond in an open bit of park. There's no park now. A new block of towers. That used to be a park though? Not a proper park, just a stretch of green with a pond on it. And sometimes there were ducks.

Perhaps not.

The past is such a strange country.

Perhaps we fed the ducks?

I can't remember.

We were always in a hurry because of him.

One tear escapes and rolls down my cheek.

I must keep going.

Who was it that we always had to please?

I turn right on to a smaller lane. I know that at its end it will open up on to a larger thoroughfare – where the timber yard is.

He was angry. He shouted.

Suddenly a tornado rises out of nowhere. It tries to push me back. A scrambled noise of voices shout: Don't go any further. You can't go there.

He'll get you.

Rehab will kick you out.

You've gone too far already.

Madness. Madness. Madness.

WHAT ARE YOU DOING?

WHAT ARE YOU DOING?

You're ugly. You're bad. You're not worth anything.

TURN AROUND. GO BACK.

HE WILL CATCH YOU.

I let the thoughts bubble up and pop and disappear.

Perhaps Fletcher is right. Perhaps I should remember who he was.

I keep walking down the narrow lane, down to the thoroughfare.

Find out and nail him. The thought spins me into panic. My knees tremble. I know on my right are the arches. Let the thought go. Focus on recovery. I hear a noise. A train is coming. The noise of trains. I'd forgotten about the noise of trains! The smell of trains. It comes at me so sharply, I must stop and lean against a lamp post. The arches are under a railway – how could I have forgotten that? The shivering in my legs spreads to somewhere deep behind my ribcage. How could I have forgotten about the train going over railway arches?

I know exactly where the room is.

But I no longer know what I'm looking for. Am I trying to find out who I am? How I ended up in that room? Why all this happened? Or to find out about the man who did such terrifying things?

Am I looking for my mother?

All I know is that I can't recover until I've stood in that room and listened to whatever it has to tell me.

The strange thing is, I don't even stop to wonder if there still is a room. Or if it's now part of somebody's flat, or whether it's locked. A force greater than reality pulls me on.

It is as if everything has always been leading to this point. The door will stand open; the room is waiting. We're linked together in some inescapable way.

And all my life I've been running from it.

58

I turn and walk along the arches under the railway. The room was never a room in a house. Fletcher was quite wrong about that. The room was a space under a railway arch. It was where he mended the cars.

I pause. Where did that memory come from?

Who was he?

And what cars did he mend?

I see him bending over an engine, the open bonnet vast and dark above him, like a monstrous bat's wing.

Something in my mind begins to wobble, like a heat haze rising off the road, fracturing the distance. A mirage forms in my mind. *Who was he?* What cars did he mend under these arches? Why did we know him?

And I walk.

My heart pumps. My breathing has gone irregular. My legs feel as if I've walked half a mile at top speed, and I'm now wading through setting concrete; a twitching starts in my calves. The bones in my knees have melted. I can barely stagger on, past the lane, past the arches. They're still being used as garage workshops.

He might still be here?

I walk down to the one at the very end, where he used to mend the cars.

Blackened brick. Uneven cobbles. Ferns growing from loose masonry. A green tinge to the windows. A mechanic inside one of the archways glances in my direction. It's not him. The mechanic takes in my figure, looks away. I'm not surprised. I remind him of death. In my Thinness he sees his own mortality.

And I so loved my Thinness.

'Don't leave me,' my Thinness murmurs.

I pat my arms, run a loving hand across my collarbone. Feel the hard roundedness beneath, the papery-thin skin above. 'I'm setting you free,' I whisper.

I don't care about the mechanic. I don't care if I'm ugly. For once, I really don't care.

I pull my jacket close around me. It's so cold.

The next two arches are locked up. Panic. At the back of my throat something tightens.

I hesitate. My resolve fails.

He might be there, waiting for you – waiting to drag you inside and lock you up all over again.

'DO IT,' orders Carmen. 'Believe in it. Complete the task. Don't chicken out like I did. Face reality. The water lily grows through the shit and the mud and the drowning to reach and flower in the light. Don't be afraid. Find the light.'

Oh, Carmen.

This is the hardest part. The drowning.

And here it is.

It's still painted that same dull racing green. The pourings of a thousand rainstorms have not washed that paint away. My memory is as clear as if time has stood still. Spreading up from the ground are those thin straggly weeds. I can't believe it. Can they possibly be the same ones? There they are, still reaching towards that wood-panelled door.

I reach out and take hold of the door handle.

I turn the handle. I push it. It's nailed shut.

I shove the door.

You see! You see! Go back!

The wood panels are rotten. I put my shoulder against the door and with all my strength I shove.

This is my time. I will not go back. I will recover.

One panel crumbles, splits.

Everything must crumble at my touch now.

Today.

No door can hold out against me. I've waited for this. With every last ounce of my will I strain against it.

The boards give.

It creaks. I yank and shove. I thrust the door handle down harder.

The door opens inwards and away from me.

There's nobody here.

I can still smell engines. I can still smell that sourness of death. It's derelict. I pause. I turn around. *What if it's not? What if he's waiting, watching?* I look back through the open door. The smell of death. I understand now. Opposite is the city abattoir. Fletcher was right about that.

I hear the lumbering of a lorry. It must be coming from beyond the wall, over there to the right.

Somebody sticks a blade into the calves of my legs. My eyes shrink and water. I stagger. I inhale sharply. I stumble back to the open door. I wheel around and around. No one is there. Somebody yanks my hair and forces my head up. I see the towers of wood, piled higher than the brick wall. Barbed wire. Through the barred window.

He's here. He's here. I know it. His shadows are stalking me.

He's not here. Just memories. I must go on. This is where all secrets end.

This is where my truth begins.

This is the workshop where he mended the cars.

I close the door behind me. I don't want to be interrupted.

Grimy light filters in, greenish, dull. There ahead, at the back of the arch, is the room.

The empty room.

I suppose it was once an office. It has a glass window with bars. It only looks out into the interior of the workshop. The glass is bubbled and opaque. I see the door.

I step around a deep pit. That's where he checked the engines. I remember standing watching. I walk towards the door. Somebody must have kicked it in. It's broken. Part of the wooden panels have sprung loose.

I push the door open.

The room is exactly as I remember.

The one armchair in the corner, its stuffing poking out. A tiny back window barred and high on the wall. Ragged carpets.

And the dead body of my mother.

59

I sink down against the armchair. One rusty spring pokes into the back of my leg.

I didn't realize she'd be here.

The tsunami is back. No warning earthquakes, no building storm. It hits. Races up the shores. I run. I scream. I'm too small to get away. My tiny legs are dragged backwards. I can't fight. A large wave forces me underwater. I gasp for breath. I gag. I scream.

I remember everything.

I remember everything.

And I can't breathe.

And my heart won't beat.

And I can't stop it from happening.

And none of it was my fault.

My mother is screaming.

And he is there.
Doing all those things again.
Drowning me.

I'm on the floor. Right where my mother lay. I can feel her very near.

Something is wrong. His shadows have dragged me under. Tony said something would be wrong. A searing pain. Potassium. I'm too weak. He called it Dani's Toxic Problems Of The Heart. The shadows. I am here. I have come this far. It must be a seizure.

My heart is in the shadows. They're curling around it. Heart failure. Sometimes it doesn't beat at all.

I should call someone.

I want to live.

He owned this garage.

Tony taught me about heart attacks.

He said he overdosed once.

Tony warned me.

My mum worked here.

I can't move. It hurts. I should dial the emergency services. It takes all the effort I have to find my phone. I drag it from my pocket. My fingers are travelling around the base of the chair leg. My palms are sweating. I fumble to swipe the phone open.

That was it. My mum worked here – in this room.

The pain comes in waves. Aching. Stabbing. I don't enter the correct passcode on my phone. I can't breathe. I try to get

281

my breath. I put my head down on the floor and suck in the earth.

Papers. She worked with all his papers.

The shadows flood forward.

He employed her. He wasn't my father. I breathe. I sip air. *I was so scared he'd be my father.*

My phone rings.

My chest has a thousand tons of concrete on it.

She just worked here. She did his paperwork. I came here with her after day care. I helped her, I think.

My phone rings again. I try to answer it.

I hope I can tell whoever is ringing to help me. I shouldn't have come here on my own. I get that now. If I die, I help nobody. My finger trembles. My chest fights back. I concentrate. I swipe the phone open.

'Hello?'

Fletcher?

Thank God. Thank God.

I can't answer. Just no air.

'Hello?' he repeats again.

'Fletch,' I whisper.

'I can't hear you very well,' he says.

I drink in water. I breathe in water. I hold the phone closer to my cheek. I press against the floor.

'Fletch,' I say.

'What's wrong?' he says.

'In the room,' I say.

'What?'

'Room,' I whisper.

'OK. Are you OK?'

'Don't know . . . Too much . . . Can't move.'

My heart. My breathing.

His voice is panicky. He tries to reassure. This is the tone he used with his mother, I just know it.

'Okaaay,' he says. 'I understand. Now listen carefully. Can you hear me?'

'Yes.'

'Just stay very, very quiet,' he says. 'Don't try to stand up. Don't even try to. Can you still hear me?'

'Yes,' I whisper.

'And don't panic,' he says. 'There is nothing to panic about. I'm going to come and help you. I'm going to put this call on hold and phone emergency services. Will you be OK while I do that?'

'No,' I whisper.

He is a life jacket holding me up. His words are a rope thrown to save me. If he leaves me, I will be alone in this empty room. Alone with the shadows. Only the sound of his voice is holding back the drowning.

'OK,' he says. 'I won't leave you right now then. We'll talk a bit. Then I must call an ambulance.'

'OK,' I whisper.

'I'm going to tell you what I've been doing. I want you to know. I want you to understand how important you are. That everything you said to me made sense. I've taken charge. I'm doing what you say. I'm doing it for me. Can you still hear me?'

'Yes,' I whisper.

283

But his voice is growing faint.

'I'm taking a bus to where you are,' he says. 'I went to a Narcotics Anonymous meeting. I went to a lot of NA meetings. In fact, I went to meetings all day. I travelled all over London and just went to meetings.'

I'm listening.

'I had to jump the buses,' he says. 'I didn't want to – it's not right. But when I have money I'll pay it all back. Are you listening?'

'Yes.'

'I'm doing OK,' he says. 'I knew I had to do it. Dani, can you hear me?'

It's hard to hang on.

'Can I put you on hold now? Can you tell me the name of the street where you are? How far is it from the woodyard?'

'No . . .'

'Just hang on. I won't go. I'm on a bus. I went to this meeting over the river,' he says. 'There were really nice guys there. People who've suffered. They understood. They welcomed me in and called me their own newcomer. They don't want to let me go. I think they saw that I want to change. I'm going to change – do you hear me, Dani?'

I can't speak any more.

'All the things you said to me. I listened. I want to be OK. You helped me to see that, Dani.'

Please just come. Please keep talking.

'One of the guys at the meeting was really kind. He said I can sleep on his sofa until I get sorted. And I called Tony. He says he'll help. He says he'll be there for me.'

I'm so glad. I'm glad Tony will help. Maybe they both need each other. Fletcher needs a dad. Tony needs a second chance at being one. I'm glad that Fletch went to the meetings. I wish he was here with me.

'How you doing, Dani?' he says. 'Can I put the call on hold now? Can you hang on while I call someone?'

I can't. I see the darkness curdling around the walls. If Fletcher stops talking, my heart stops beating.

The shadows are slithering around in the corners of the room. It's like the Alien told me it is. The outer darkness. It was always there behind everything.

The black hole. It will suck me up, and I will be nothing. Without the Alien there to protect me, I cannot hold back the darkness. And the Alien is mad at me. He won't save me any more. The Alien is sitting on his star in Outer Space, waiting for me to join him.

'Don't go,' I say.

'Listen, Dani,' says Fletcher. 'I really need to call the emergency services. I'm off the bus and I'm walking down the high street in Clapham. I'm getting on another bus but the Tube or trains would be quicker. I can get to you quicker if you can let me go.'

I know who the man is. I want to tell Fletcher. We can find him. We can bring him to justice. We can live in the light. We can kill the shadows. But not now. Right now I just need Fletcher.

'Can you hang on while I do that?'

I can't let Fletcher go. He's the silver thread that's holding me to this world; without him, without hearing that he's on his way, winding the thread in, without hearing his voice, I cannot hold on to my heart. It's like he's there inside my heart. He's one of its strings and he's pulling all its chambers together and keeping the blood pumping.

'OK,' he says. 'I understand.'

And that's the thing: he does understand. I don't need to explain to him. He knows if the thread isn't cut, I can hold on.

'Just keep talking,' I whisper into the phone.

'But you're all the way over in Lewisham,' he says. 'The bus is going to take for ever. And I don't know the streets around there. It might take me hours.'

Holding on and letting go.

'OK,' he says. 'I'm going to do something illegal.'

I don't know what to say. I don't know if legalities apply any more, when you're lying on the floor in the empty room where your mother died.

'I don't have any money,' he says, 'so if I'm going to jump the buses, I might as well jump a taxi.'

I don't understand.

'I'm going to flag down a London cab and get him to drive me all the way to you. It'll be much quicker.'

'But . . .' I whisper. It's too much. Just get here.

'Don't worry,' he says. 'I'll have to do a basher when we get to the other end.'

I don't know what a basher is. Fletcher tells me anyway.

'You have to do these things when you're an addict on the streets.' He laughs. 'What it means is, I get the taxi to stop near an ATM because I claim I don't have enough cash on me. The taxi pulls up and I get out and then I do a basher. I quickly bash the pavement with my feet in a direction that is not back towards the taxi.'

He laughs again. 'And he'll be pulled up out of sight or on a red line or facing the wrong way – so he can't follow. When you live on the streets you know how to do this kind of stuff – you even know the best ATM machines to get the taxi to pull up at. You know the ones near an alley you can escape down, the ones with no cameras and no stopping and no parking for miles.'

One shadow is sneaking a tentacle out towards me.

'I'm gonna try it now. If he follows me, I don't care anyway,' Fletcher says.

I hear him yell, 'Taxi!'

I hear an engine. I hear a car door slam.

I hear somebody say, 'Where to?'

I hear Fletcher say, 'Lewisham. Phoenix Wharf, Mordly Hill Street.'

Then he says to me, 'You have to tell me exactly how to get to where you are from the woodyard. Can you do that, Dani?'

I don't know if I can.

'It's the arches,' I whisper. 'Go down the arches. Last one. The street behind the woodyard. Train line.'

I hear traffic. The noise of a radio.

'OK,' he says. 'I'll go down the arches.' He sounds unsure.

'You're going to be OK,' says Carmen.

She is standing with my mother, very near me, by a door I've never noticed before.

And I look up.

I see my mother's face.

It feels like the very first time.

And it's her. It really is.

'My baby,' she whispers.

She moves across the room. She sits down on the floor beside me. She strokes my hair, kisses my forehead. She cradles my head and I feel her loving Thinness.

Through the strange doorway, I can see a greenish light.

My mother says, 'Don't let go, my baby. Don't go through that door. I love you.'

I hear Fletcher ask the driver if he'll stop at an ATM. I hear him spin the driver a line. He's so convincing. Fletcher is coming. I hear a car door. A swishing noise.

'Can't talk . . . nearly there . . .'

A breathlessness. A wavering. The tentacles curl forward.

Fletcher is coming.

I can no longer hear his voice very well.

'Hang on.'

I seem to be fading in and out. I want to hang on, but the shadows won't wait. The cold of Outer Space has already touched me. The doorway seems suddenly wider. I'm freezing. Only my mother's love is keeping me alive. Fletcher's voice is very dim and very far away.

I cradle the phone into my ear, just trying to hear him. His voice comes in snatches. I hear the lorries of the timber yard, cracking, smacking. Their gates squeal open; I'm back, far away in the past. I reach out to touch my mother's leg and it is as cold as Pluto.

'HANG ON,' Fletcher shouts. 'I can hear you breathing.'

Fletcher.

'I'm coming.' He's panting. 'I'm on the bash now.' Gasps of air. 'Only two streets away. Hang on.'

But the shadows of cold have touched me. The Alien is rocking on his star, laughing. All his tentacles reach out to embrace me. And that silver line to Fletcher's phone is so stretched.

'Found the arches,' Fletcher screams down the phone. 'Where exactly are you?'

I can't answer.

'OK, I'm here – last arch,' yells Fletcher.

I can hear him. *Really hear him, not just through the phone.* Voice stretched. Panting.

Really hear him.

So far away.

'I'm calling an ambulance. I'm here. I'll shout. I'm still talking to you.'

His voice fades.

'I'm HERE.'

I hear him say the address then, 'Collapse. Ambulance. Hurry.'

'The very last arch looks empty,' he shouts.

Yes, everywhere is empty. The darkness in the carpet is pressing against my cheek. I'm so cold.

My mother soothes my brow and whispers, 'I'm so sorry, my darling.'

Carmen smiles at me. 'I'm waiting for you, when you've made up your mind.'

I blink at her.

'It's the only final way to solve the dilemma,' she says.

289

60

'Dani, say something!'
 Fletcher.
 I think I am saying something?
 But I can't answer.

In the distance I hear a wailing.

STEP TWELVE
SPIRITUAL AWAKENING

61

The wail of emergency services.

They're coming.

My mother smiles at me. I can feel her love, warm like sunshine.

'Oh, Dani,' Fletcher says.

He's a shell now, fragile as a dried sea urchin.

'Don't die,' he says.

His eyes pass through me, pass through the walls of the empty room and out over London.

'You're the only one who makes any sense.' His voice hollows out. 'I need you. I can get better. I can get clean.'

'OK,' I whisper.

And I mean it.

Because here I am, back in the room with my mother, and she loves me and she wants me to live.

And that is the thing about love. It has a power beyond anything in the universe and all black holes shun it.

Sarah Mussi

And it doesn't matter any more who locked that door on the empty room, or how our mothers died.

Or who that third person was. Or why he did what he did. He can wait. We will find him out. Now is not his time.

Not really.

That will come.

Fletcher is here.

There will always be third persons to face. We can leave them behind. We will leave him behind. Let them face their own karma.

Our addictions were third people.

Let them go.

Our very own third people.

Just like my Alien.

But we no longer have to give anything power over us any more.

'You'll help me?' Fletcher asks.

'Yes.'

'To beat this thing?'

'Yes.'

'All the way?'

'Yes.'

'Whatever I do?'

'Yes.'

And I will. I will.

That's all. I will.

My Fletcher.

I will be there for him, even unto death.

Fletcher sighs like, at last, he can breathe. He takes my

hand. He kisses the back of my fingers. I know what he's saying. His kiss tells me that he will be there for me too.

All the way.

Through the black hole of Outer Space.

A shiver runs up my arm.

It's bright in here. My mother kisses me and holds out her arms to Fletcher. Carmen smiles at us. It feels real. It feels good. I've grown tired of the cold of Outer Space.

Way too much darkness.

Fletcher feels it too. He laughs, straightens up.

The Alien shrugs and rolls his eyes, like he's lost at a game of tiddlywinks. I'm so glad he's not going to be mad. He pulls a torch out of a huge sucker and spotlights us.

Light spills all around.

Then he waves goodbye with all his tentacles and walks out of the doorway, which is now as wide as wide can be. Through its reaches I see distant galaxies. He bows once. He's gone.

I know it's for good.

The light stays pooling everywhere.

'We'll live, one day at a time.' says Fletcher. 'Just for each other then.'

'If I don't make it . . .' I whisper.

'You will make it,' he says.

'And you?'

He smiles.

'You're goddamn right,' he says.

Acknowledgements

Joanna Bateson-Hill
Adrienne Dines
Ruth Eastham
Roisin Heycock
Sophie Hicks
Caroline Johnson
Melissa L. N.A. Speaker for her inspiring share
Paul Nash
Sarah Odedina
Madeleine Stevens
B.J.M.
The internet
Al-Anon UK
CoDA UK
UKNA
And everyone at Oneworld.